THE MADDY SAGA

BOOK EIGHT

I0525543

PONYGIRL PLEASURES

BY

PAUL BLADES

Cover Art by Agnes Knox
agnes.knox@gmail.com

Dark Visions Publications
darkvisionspub@gmail.com

Previously published:

Vol. I   Maddy becomes a Ponygirl
Vol. II   The Training of a Ponygirl
Vol. III   Ponygirl Champion
Vol. IV   Ponygirl Summer
Vol. V   Ponygirl Love
Vol. VI   Ponygirl Season
Vol. VII   Ponygirl Gambit

Watch for publication of the other books in the Maddy Saga:

Vol. IX   Ponygirl Peril
Vol. X   Ponygirl's Choice

Other books by Paul Blades:

Klitzman's Isle
Klitzman's Empire
Klitzman's Paradise
Klitzman's Pawn Part One
Klitzman's Pawn Part Two
Slaver's Dozen- A Tale of Klitzman's Isle
The Taking of Cheryl Part One
The Taking of Cheryl Part Two: Slaver's Bait
Comfort Girl No. 4
Sacrifice to the Emerald God
The Blue Cantina: Anna's Surrender
The Warlord's Concubine, Books 1, 2, 3 and 4
Dreams and Desires, Books 1 and 2
Carmella Condemned

CHAPTER ONE
A LUNCH AT KHALID'S

The women had been waiting patiently, or maybe not so patiently, in the courtyard for the better part of an hour. Maleef Bardooji, however, was in no hurry. He was supping at the sumptuous and fabled lunch table of Khalid Rashini, the foremost slaver in all of Kalikastan. The rotund native of this outlaw country was renowned for his cuisine. There had been a first course of Black Sea prawns sautéed lightly in garlic, butter and lemon followed by a strong flavored cabbage soup. The main course was a tender, braised veal chop highlighted by a pungent mushroom sauce, delicious, fresh picked and gently steamed, dark green peas mixed with dainty pearl onions and razor thin slivers of almonds. The potatoes had been roasted in olive oil and garlic with a hint of rosemary. And the wine, a dark red Kazuli from Khalid's own vineyard had had just the right combination of fruitiness and tartness, a rival to the great Merlots of California.

Maleef was a buyer for one of the better known training centers in Kalikastan and he was on his bi-weekly tour of the import houses for new stock. Khalid was his cousin, twice removed. While the Russians had seemed to take over everything else, the slaving trade had remained mostly a native industry. It took a fine, well developed eye to determine which of the imported young females would acclimate themselves most favorably to their new roles in life. Kalikastani tribesmen had been in the business of kidnapping and selling women for centuries, Ukrainians to the Russians, Russians to the Turks, Rumanians to the Hungarians and Poles to everybody.

The country was ideally situated for trade with its many neighbors. It was small, but not too small that a brace of females captured from a caravan couldn't be whisked away into the hills before the Czar's cavalrymen could catch them. Even during the Great Patriotic War they had been able to keep up a brisk trade of Russian and German nurses captured on the battlefield and woeful, but still attractive, female refugees and displaced persons. When the Red Army overran the Reich, they had brought back truckloads of them. But the postwar resurgence of Communism and the deadly bureaucratization of the country had brought the river of females that flowed to the small Soviet Socialist Republic to a virtual trickle.

The fall of the Soviet Union had brought a rebirth of the industry. The liberal democratic republic of Kalikastan lasted about seven months. A coup financed by Russian gangsters had brought the fledgling democracy tumbling down and it had been off to the races ever since. Maleef's clan had started one of the first official training houses. Its license from the autocratic, gangster run government had the number '3' embossed on it in gold. Maleef had only been 20 years old at the time and had had to work his way up from, in effect, a stable boy, washing and cleaning out the cages and cells in which the unhappy young girls made their homes while being broken in, to an assistant trainer, then a trainer. He had been promoted to become an assistant buyer just after his twenty-fifth birthday. He now was the head of that department at 34.

The plates had been removed from their luncheon repast by the two pretty, naked slave girls that Khalid kept on as part of his regular staff. As you would expect, they were beautiful in face and body. Khalid had the pick of the crop, of course, and he would be expected to choose for his servants the most appealing of the young females that came through his facility. One was a tall redhead. She had round, firm breasts and large, well toned thighs. Her bush had been trimmed to a little beard over her plump love lips. Her mouth was saucy, almost impertinent and her dark brown eyes were round and flashed a submerged hatred of the men who ordered her around so churlishly. Her reddish brown hair was full and curly and reached down to just below her ears.

The other girl was slender and shorter. She had pale skin and starry, blue eyes. Her hair was black and long, down to the middle of her back. Her breasts were smaller than the other girl's, but were more than a handful, and curved upwards slightly at the ends. Her nipples were sharp as pencil points and she had a dark maroon areola surrounding each one. Her loins had been completely denuded and Maleef had enjoyed caressing her smooth, pale love lips each time she had leaned over the table to deliver a platter, to refill the large, round wine glasses, or to remove the men's leavings.

The women had just come into the dining room with dessert and coffee. The dessert was a soft, rich, rainbow sherbet scooped into a large ball into a small silver bowl. The coffee was thick and strong, virtually an espresso. As the red headed girl set the coffee urn down on the table after pouring his cup, Maleef leaned forward and took hold of one of her full, meaty breasts. He felt the girl stiffen with resentment, but she did not move away. Maleef brought her nipple to his mouth and took it between his lips while running his soft, delicate, knowledgeable hand down her thigh. She spread her legs obediently and the slave buyer slipped his hand over her plump mons and then slid his longest finger along the length of her slit. It took a few moments for the girl to lubricate herself, but he was quickly able to slide the finger deeply into her and then, after gathering her moisture, run it up to the tiny digit at the apex of her sex.

The girl's body soon softened as she stood next to her assailant. She uttered a low sigh as she dutifully allowed the man's hand to excite her. Maleef expected nothing less. Khalid would not have allowed undisciplined slave girls to serve his honored guest. The man shifted his oral attentions to the girl's other breast, sucking in the stiffened, fat nipple while continuing to tease her moistened gash. He broke for air when the girl exuded a deep moan.

"Would you like to fuck her?" Khalid asked politely. He was pleased that his guest had found his slave girl enticing enough to enjoy her flesh. It was a matter of simple politeness, of course, to complement the owner by giving in to his slave girls' allure. Khalid would expect nothing less from Maleef, the most knowledgeable and refined buyer of female flesh in the country. But he could tell that the redheaded girl had indeed sparked the buyer's somewhat jaded lust and that his interest in her flesh was authentic and not a bow to courtesy.

"Ahhhh, not today, Khalid," Maleef replied sorrowfully. He was casually dressed: black, well pressed slacks, shiny, hand tooled, black loafers and a cerise colored, knit polo shirt. On its pocket was emblazoned a snarling mountain lion, the symbol of his training house, a design that would by tomorrow evening adorn the bellies of the women that he purchased today. The tattoo on a female slave's belly proclaimed her training house wherever she went, a permanent testament to the rigors and efficacy of her training and where to return her for cruel, painful reinforcement of her dedication to her duties if she forgot them, free of charge, of course. After she had been broken in for a day or two, her individual trainer would select her new slave name, which would then be tattooed on her upper chest above her breasts in two inch high, blue, Cyrillic letters

Maleef reluctantly released the heavily breathing redhead. "I got a late start today and I had to skip a few stops," he explained politely. "I wanted to make sure that I could enjoy your wonderful lunch and so I interrupted my schedule to come here. But if she's still here when I come back in two weeks, I'll take you up on it. She has a surliness that appeals to me. Is she American?"

The men were speaking in their native patios, a language that the women were sure not to understand, but her owner's invitation and the buyer's responses were not lost on the red headed girl. She was waiting for permission to resume her duties and gave the black haired man a look of hatred.

"No," Khalid replied. "German, believe it or not. I've had her about a month. If you're interested in her I'll put her through her paces."

"No," Maleef answered. "I don't think so. She's beautiful, but I'm looking for a certain type today, to fill some special requests. But, if we have time, I'll be happy to take a second look at her." He ran his hand over her plump rear globes while watching her fiery eyes. "She would be a treat to train."

"Later, then maybe," Khalid said. "Let's finish our dessert and I'll show you what I have for you today."

Khalid and Maleef scooped out large spoonfuls of the cold, soft, fruity substance from their bowls and downed large sips of their coffees. The redheaded slave girl joined her sister standing off on the side. The dining room was a comfortable size, about 20' by 20', and decorated in a man's style with large, heavy, dark oak furniture. The table was about 10' around and was dressed with a simple, white, cotton cloth. The ceiling was high and a black, wrought iron chandelier sat over the table. The women stood attentively at the side of the room in the gap between the long, heavily grained credenza and the breakfront from which they had retrieved the thick, ceramic plates and bowls for the men's meal. Their backs were straight and their eyes focused downwards, their hands crossed behind their backs so as not to hide their charms. They both wore leather collars around their necks and leather bracelets around their wrists and ankles, standard equipage for slave girls. Their bellies and chests were unmarred, however, for Khalid didn't have the time or the inclination to actually train the sluts that he selected as his private servants. He grew tired of them quickly and sold them off or gifted them away. There were always plenty of beautiful new subjects to choose from.

Maleef slurped off the last remnants of his sherbet from his small silver spoon and scooted down the dregs of his coffee. "Ahhhhhhhh," he intoned. He looked over to the slave girls. The redhead and the black haired girl were bookending a somewhat plump, distraught girl with wavy brown hair and large breasts. She had a large triangle of wild, furry, brown pubic hair between her thighs. Unlike the two servants, she did not wear slave regalia. Her hands were tied behind her with leather thongs. Her mouth was covered by a leather shield that was tied behind her head. She had been standing there obediently with watery eyes and a furrowed brow throughout the meal. Each time that she had shifted her balance while waiting tremulously for orders from the men, her heavy breasts had swayed and shimmered delightfully.

Maleef made it a rule never to inspect slave flesh without first taking his sexual edge off. It didn't do to be seduced by pleasant lips or a luscious snatch. He had to consider the whole female in his appraisals. "Do you mind?" he asked the heavyset, black bearded slaver.

"Of course not," was the polite reply.

Maleef made motion for the brown haired girl to approach him. She had long red stripes across her belly, breasts and thighs and Maleef knew that the girl had already been taught the rudiments of her new profession. He could use the mouth of one of the serving sluts, but Khalid had made a point of producing the big breasted girl for their luncheon and he wanted to sample her.

The girl approached hesitatingly. Her body was trembling and her firm, heavy breasts shuddered as she advanced. Maleef had turned his chair to her and he pointed to the floor in front of him. Emitting a high pitched, barely audible whine, the girl sank to her knees in front of the suave looking man. He reached over and removed her gag, drawing the thick leather plug that was attached to the shield from inside her mouth, and tossed it on the table. Her plump lips were trembling and the wetness of her red rimmed eyes had produced two tears that flowed slowly down her cheeks. Maleef smiled.

It was always a pleasure to use a female who was still not yet inured to her new role in life. There was something about their shame at submitting so readily to their new masters' demands, as if they should be resisting their fate worse than death with all of their body and soul. But transported hundreds of miles, if not thousands, from their homes, reduced to the status of chattel, bound and beaten, confined, used, deprived of voice and rendered powerless regarding their fates, what choice did they really have? The fact that all of the women around them had succumbed, were equally naked and subservient prisoners, and watching those that protested or exhibited the slightest evidence of rebellion be brutally whipped before their very eyes, made resistance to their fates seem pointless.

Seeing that the young, frightened girl was ready for him, Maleef undid the zipper to his neatly pressed trousers and removed his long, thick cock from its hiding place. It had already started to harden in anticipation of the girl's services. He held it out to her and urged her on with the English words for 'suck my cock'. English was the lingua franca for slave girls. Coming from so many lands, it was necessary to teach them a common tongue for the few words they would need to fulfill their duties. Keeping them ignorant for the most part of Russian, the most common language extant in Kalikastan since the takeover, or Kalikastani, made sense. This way you could have a perfectly uninhibited conversation in front of them without worrying that they would know what you were talking about.

The girl gave a frantic, sideways look at Khalid. It was he who had laid the lash to her earlier that day, soon after her arrival in this hellish place. He had already taken possession of her mouth and the slit between her thighs. The girl had no idea where she was and the reality of her situation had not yet fully sunk in. She knew what the black haired man wanted though and, remembering the fat man's cruel treatment of her a short while ago, needed no convincing to obey him.

A week or so ago, the pretty, but slightly plump, 20 year old Deidre Murphy had been at a beach party in Panama City, Florida. It was a late September fling. She and a few of her friends, juniors at the University of Pennsylvania, had taken advantage of a long weekend, none of them had classes on Fridays or Mondays, those classes were for ignorant underclassmen, and had driven down to the Florida panhandle to get some sun and have some fun. They had met some boys on the beach and been invited back to their house for some beers and a little coke.

Dressed in her bright red one piece, she didn't consider herself to have the figure for bikinis like her three friends, Deidre remembered taking in a long line of the pretty, white powder. She remembered little else until she awoke in a tiny little cage naked, bound and gagged. She had cried for hours until some women came and loaded her and her friends up in a brown delivery van marked "National Uniform Company" and hauled her away. They had spent hours and hours locked into narrow lockers in the truck's interior until they were finally released and held in a dismal basement lined with cages, each containing a bound and hooded woman. She had been hooded too and then, after many more hours, taken out and given an injection. She awoke inside a long aluminum container, here, where she was now being held, a few hours ago. She had been whipped, her mouth and sex raped. Whatever was going to happen to her, she wanted to make sure that she was not whipped again. It had been excruciating. Until she could figure out some way to get free, she would do whatever the cruel men who held her prisoner said.

The brown haired girl edged herself closer to the tall, thin but well built man's cock. She could feel her oversized breasts sway and jerk as she moved on her knees. The man had spread his legs widely and she leaned over hesitatingly, trying to delay the moment when the fat penis pierced her lips. It wasn't that she had anything against blow jobs. Quite the contrary. But the thought of being made into some kind of whore or sex slave made her mind fill with despair. It wasn't what she wanted. But what she wanted didn't seem to matter anymore.

Maleef sighed as the girl's plump lips subsumed his meat. She deftly gobbled the helmet of his prick between her lips and gave it a soft, practiced suck. He felt her tongue roll along the thin, pinkish glans underneath the head and then over the tiny slit at his cock's tip. He looked down at the brown haired head between his thighs and placed a hand on it, urging it forward. The girl gave a moan of dismay and then leaned closer to him, sliding her broad lips down the length of his prick.

"Ahhhhhhhhhhhh," Maleef sighed as he felt the moist heat of the girl's mouth transfer to his manhood. The lips of the newly enslaved girl dragged slowly down his pole as the tongue inside her mouth continued to swirl and dance along it. She did not hurry at her task like most new slave girls did, anxious to have the odious task behind them, but seemed to luxuriate in the act like it had been, in her former life, one of her hobbies. Her hands, locked behind her with a leather strap, were tightly clenched and strained at their bindings, evidence of the girl's unhappiness despite her skillful attention to her duty. She raised and lowered her head, giving the man's cock a warm, lust driving bath, lingering each time at the bulbous head and then slurping downwards again to its very base.

It did not take too long for Maleef's passions to rise towards explosion. He closed his eyes and leaned his head back the better to languish in the exquisite sensations. His hands gripped the girl's head firmly and he began to urge her to rapidity. She took the hint and began to slurp her way up and down his pole quickly, moaning and whining unhappily. When his cock began to jet its piquant sauce into her mouth, she gave out a muffled cry but did not falter in her efforts. Maleef groaned as his cock danced in her mouth, his thighs stiffening and his hands gripping ever so much more tightly on the pleasure giving head.

When his cock's convulsions ebbed, he allowed the girl's head to rise from his loins. Her face was awash with tears and her plump lips trembled as if she were about to break into uncontrollable sobs. Maleef patted her on her head and laughed.

"You old devil!" he exclaimed at the slave trader. "I knew you had her here for a reason."

Khalid smiled, ever the salesman. He knew that the buyer would probably bypass the purchase of this somewhat dumpy American. The girls she came with were all prime specimens. She was just a little wide in the beam and had a small roll of fat around her waist, nothing that a strict regimen of training couldn't correct. But when she sucked his cock that morning, he realized she was something special. If she was this good now, she would be world class when she was trained. He knew that he had his cousin hooked.

'Okay, Okay," Maleef laughed. "I'll take her. Have her put in my van." He patted the brown haired girl's head. One of Khalid's men, who had been standing around the room dutifully during the minibanquet, stepped up and restored the girl's gag. He unceremoniously took hold of her arm and pulled her to her feet and then towards the door.

Something had just happened. The former Deidre knew it. Had she been sold? Was that it? In her efforts to avoid a whipping had she done too good a job? What would happen to her now?

The young, American, former college student would have plenty of time to ruminate on her future. Khalid's man hauled her out the door and would soon have her crouched in one of the little cages in Maleef's van.

It was just past 2 o'clock in the afternoon when the men stepped out of the door to Khalid's suite and onto the walkway on the second floor of the structure. The massive building, constructed from roughly hewn stone, was a former military fortress from the days when the Czar's troops were required to keep the unruly Kalikastani tribesmen on a short leash. It was shaped in the form of a 'u', with squared off corners. The first floor consisted of the slave barracks, a kitchen, the guards' offices, a lounge for the men, a discipline room and other facilities related to the maintenance and control of his stock and their preparation for sale. The second floor contained his offices and apartment, rooms for guests, apartments for the senior supervisors and administrative space. At the mouth of the 'u' was a large stone wall with a huge, arched, double hung door big enough to allow trucks to enter and leave and thick enough to withstand an 18th century canon ball, at least one fired from some distance away. In the middle was the courtyard, about 200' on each side and paved with cobblestones. There were various posts mounted around it for securements purposes and a small section devoted to the parking of cars belonging to customers and guests.

Most of Khalid's customers were, like Maleef, of the wholesale variety. Khalid needed to turn over his stock quickly, as he received ten to twenty of the sluts per week. But there was a certain class of buyer, friends of the ruling Commission, the various clan and gang leaders, rich industrialists from Russia or the Ukraine, who were permitted private showings. Typically, they would make their selection and have the girl shipped out to one of the training houses. For it was a strict regulation that no slave girl be permitted to serve the public until she had undergone a rigorous course of training. This cut down on escape attempts and the problem of dealing with recalcitrant or unruly sluts. Once a slave girl hit one of the many whorehouses in the country or was delivered to a wealthy businessman or to one of the estates outside the capital, she was pretty much acclimated to, if not happy with, her new status.

It was a warm fall day and the sun beat down on the frightened, naked women who had been standing at attention in the courtyard for the last hour and a half. There were 25 of them, not all of the fresh slaves presently housed in the slave barracks, but most of them. A few had been held back as being not ready to be sold off for one reason or another or were being held for special buyers. The women had been rousted from the barracks and made to stand in five rows. While in their stalls it was customary to have their hands bound behind them and their necks attached to a chain anchored in the wall. Each stall contained a long padded bench built in to it on which the newly enslaved, naked, pretty young girl could sit or lay while awaiting her eating or exercise period, or on which any one of the many, callous, male guards could fuck her.

For presentation purposes, the unhappy women's hands had been untied from behind their backs and the leather strap wound around their necks. Their hands had then been tied to the ends of the straps, raising their arms, elbows out, and making their naked breasts jut out nicely. They were required to stand with their feet apart and their backs erect. Khalid preferred the use of leather straps to confine the newly imbonded women. It was so much more satisfying to tie off a woman's hands behind her back or to her neck than to clip together a pair of cuffs. Also, the sensation of feeling the leather being pulled tightly around her wrists and callously tied off gave the frightened, disoriented female a greater appreciation of her helplessness and the power of the men who now controlled her.

Maleef squinted his eyes to adjust them to the bright light of the afternoon and then looked down on the presented pulchritude. His body had a warm glow from his recent orgasm and his belly was tight and satisfied from his sumptuous meal. The women looked tired from their ordeal in the sun. As one, they looked up apprehensively at the men emerging on the veranda above them. Their gags had been loosened and hung down on their chests, ready for quick and efficient installation after their bodies had been examined. Blonds, brunettes, redheads, girls with hair as black as night, all stood ready to submit to evaluation, not sure whether being selected would be a good thing or a bad.

The two men strolled casually down the stairs. At the bottom, there was a post and a tall, wide shouldered female was affixed to it by a chain to a broad, rough, leather collar around her neck. Her head was covered with a leather hood that had tiny vertical slits for her eyes. Her chestnut colored hair emerged from its back, fastened into a ponytail. Her feet were booted and locked spread out, attached to rings that had been pounded into the ground. Her hands were affixed behind her and she was gagged.

Maleef took a moment to examine her. She was good ponygirl stock, although his house did not deal in such creatures. She had thick, solid thighs and large breasts. As Maleef approached her, her head tilted slightly, anxious to find out what new torment or cruel treatment was in store for her. She whined and shook her imprisoned body as he measured the heft of her breasts and ran his hand over her smooth, flat belly. Her pussy had been denuded of hair and he gave her prominent love lips a slight squeeze.

"So how is the ponygirl trade going?" Maleef asked Khalid casually as he fondled the former woman.

"Very good indeed," Khalid replied. "Although, it's always hard to get good stock. Ever since the Americans got involved, the sport has really taken off. There are three new estates that formed this summer and two more awaiting approval from the Commission."

"Ah," Maleef said, "the Americans. You refer to Mr. Burnham, of course."

"Naturally," Khalid replied. "He has brought in several boatloads of money and has made some connections for new sources of product."

Michael Burnham was a self made billionaire who had recently been admitted into the insular country and allowed to establish his own estate up north. He had his own stable of ponygirls and was running his own slave training house. He was also a source of a steady supply of unhappy young women from the States. Deidre, although she didn't know it, was one of his imports. Burnham had made a deal with Khalid and now received a piece of the action on young girls brought in through connections he had established in Latin and South America and the Caribbean as well as China and Southeast Asia. And he had opened up some export markets as well. Since 9/11, the countries in the Middle East had been under strict surveillance and it was harder and harder for them to bring in new girls. Burnham had made arrangements for special flights to those countries direct from Kalikastan which, because it permitted certain American security organizations to operate interrogation centers and prisons in the country, had cleared Burnham's shipments, sight unseen.

"I have to be frank," Maleef said. "Although business has benefited greatly from Mr. Burnham's activities, I don't trust the Americans. I don't believe that they have the staying power to keep up their end of the business and I don't like the idea of their agents wandering through the country."

Khalid was making money hand over fist from Burnham's marketing efforts and had nothing but good to say about the man.

"I can assure you that Mr. Burnham knows just what he is doing. And as to the CIA and other agencies, well, they have reason to keep us happy. The war on terror, as they call it, will go on forever. It's big business for everybody. It's good, too, to have someone to counterbalance Russia in case it ever gets the idea to reannex our little people's republic. And then there's the pipeline."

Burnham had essentially bought his way into the country by bidding on and winning the contract to construct a huge oil and gas pipeline through Kalikastan. It was all being paid for a by a consortium of Western European governments and everybody stood to make millions. Burnham had promised to spread the subsidiary contracts for materials and workmen around as well as a large share of the graft. Wherever worker's camps had sprung up, there had also appeared, overnight, brothels, saloons and gambling joints all licensed by the Kalikastani Ruling Commission. The work would take years.

What neither Khalid nor any of the Ruling Commission knew was that Burnham's admission to the country had been based on false pretenses. Last spring, his favorite niece, Madeline, had been kidnapped and transported to Kalikastan and turned into a ponygirl. And a very successful one at that. Burnham had hired Jake Barnes, an efficient and ruthless fixer, to track Maddy down after her kidnapping and the trail had led through a slaving operation in Elizabeth, New Jersey direct to Kalikastan. There was no way to trace her ultimate fate from outside the country and no way in for most law abiding, normal people to enter it. And so Jake had come up with a plan.

They seized control of the Jersey slaving operation and, posing as gangsters, had convinced the powers that be in this small but prosperous haven for ne'er do wells to let Burnham establish an estate here. That was, of course, after Burnham had won the pipeline contract and dangled hundreds of millions of dollars in profits before their eyes. They found Maddy all right, but Burnham, having been seduced by the outrageous lifestyle he found here, had 'gone native', so to speak, and nixed any plans for a quick rescue and flight from the country. Burnham would do nothing to unduly jeopardize his status in Kalikastan. He had moved the nucleus of his corporate headquarters here, acquired his very own ponygirl herd and a bevy of compliant, subservient slave girls. And he was now neck deep in the international trade in kidnapped females and various other forms of contraband.

Maleef continued to fondle the loins of the new ponygirl until her pussy had lubricated and she gave out a frustrated moan, shaking her hips as if she could evade his torments. The slave buyer smiled. "She's passionate," he commented.

"Yes, a good selection. She's due to be picked up later today. I know your House does not train ponygirls, but I heard that your cousin does. Is this true?"

Almost every Kalikastani was related to every other one. The term 'cousin' had come to denote a close working friendship. Maleef was wiping his moisture laden hand on the new ponygirl's breasts. "Yes, Artouf," he replied. "He trains them down in the South. He breaks them in and then sells them to the estates that need to fill in their racing card or who don't do training themselves. It's too bad you sold this one. He's always looking for new ponies."

"Well, I believe I have a nice, blond, American ponygirl coming in in a week or so. If you want, as a courtesy to you, I'll hold her for him. Top dollar though, agreed?"

Maleef knew better than to argue money with Khalid. Although bargaining was second nature to their culture, this was one area where you either took the price or left it. Khalid was fair and never gouged. And if you wanted little favors like this one, you paid what Khalid demanded.

"I would be obliged," Maleef said, bowing slightly to the slave dealer. He gave the distraught, new ponygirl a pat on her breasts and he moved off.

Khalid did not disturb the slave girl buyer while he was inspecting the merchandise. He devoted all of his senses to his task and had a natural eye for the best. Before making a close inspection of any of them, he walked slowly and calmly down the lines of naked, presented women, looking them over carefully and making mental notes to himself. From time to time he squeezed a breast or tested a thigh. When he had gone through them all, he reversed course, pointing first to this one and to that and saying, "No....No....No...." Two of Khalid's men followed the expert and as each girl was rejected, quickly reinstalled her gag and dragged her out of line. One of his other men then whipped her ass with a short, leather quirt, making the girl squeal and forcing her to run back into the barracks.

Maleef, besides keeping a general eye out for promising females, was looking for a particular type. A customer was opening up a restaurant in Dlitski, the capital, and wanted to staff it with slight, fragile looking girls, preferably blond. He was looking for girls with an ephemeral look, clear, pale skin, small hands and dainty breasts. And they needed to be able to take a whip well. Not just absorbing pain, but having flesh on which the marks would stand out prettily. So they had to have a strong character to endure the daily infliction of abuse, and unmarred, perfect skin.

He walked up to the first, unhappy, frightened girl, a lanky blond with tea cup sized breasts and long, languorous legs. She had a long sexual slit surrounded by narrowly trimmed, pale, pussy hair. Her eyes filled with tears as Maleef measured and weighed her breasts, squeezed her narrow hips with his hands and took stock of her long, trim thighs. He had her bend over so that he could examine her rear and explore her sex. Once she had lubricated to his satisfaction, he had her stand up again and gave each of her now stiff nipples a long suck. He looked in her mouth and examined every inch of her for scars or marks such as moles or birthmarks. He had already rejected the girls who wore tattoos. Unfortunately for them, their decisions to mar their flesh had probably condemned them to the meanest of the brothels in the capital. The better places wanted girls whose bodies were a clean slate.

Once done with the blond, Maleef moved on. After he had looked closely at all the girls and rejected some out of hand, he went back through the line and rejected some more. "No….No….No…." he continued until there was only eleven of the original twenty five women left. He had rejected the first blond he had looked at. Her nose was just a little too long and her mouth a tad too small. The ones that were left were prime candidates, though. Three of the girls would fit the bill for his client nicely. And the others were beautiful as well.

Now the real tests began. He slapped their faces and pulled harshly at their nipples to gauge their reactions. He squeezed their dainty love lips tightly until they moaned with pain. Some of the women would cry and scream at the least application of force to their bodies. These he made a note to reject. Not only was it irksome to have a slave girl caterwauling at the slightest provocation, but the female needed to have a high tolerance for pain for good training. As his mentor had taught him when he was first getting to know the ropes, you had to get to the learning zone, the place where the pain was so intolerable, so excruciating, that the female would do anything to avoid a repetition. Girls who could not get there without falling into hysterical, nearly psychotic reactions were not accepted by the better houses.

Eleven crying, terrorized females stood in the court-yard, awaiting the tall, black haired man's judgment. Maleef pointed to two of them, uttering, "No....No." The girls were hustled back to the barracks swiftly. That left nine. He had decided to limit himself to seven females, and he already had one, the oral specialist Khalid had proffered to him after lunch. He would need one more test.

The experienced slave buyer stood back and gave Khalid a nod. Khalid issued a curt order to his men and, at their command, the girls all pealed off and commenced to run at full speed around the circumference of the courtyard. It was an exercise that they performed several times a day while awaiting a purchaser at Khalid's. He liked to keep them in good shape for showings, and it prevented them from becoming too morose while wiling their time away in their stalls through much of the day.

Maleef and Khalid watched the barefooted girls make their rounds, their hands still tied around heir necks, their pretty breasts swaying and jerking as they ran, their hair flying about their heads. Some of Khalid's men insured their enthusiastic cooperation with their whips as they went along and there would be the occasional squeal of pain as one of them began to slow her pace. Normally, the girls ran with their hands tied behind them and wearing their gags. And so the pretty, young women struggled to keep their balance as they sprinted along in this new position, hands held high above their shoulders.

"I have some Chinese girls coming in next week," Khalid mentioned to Maleef as the girls continued their terrorized, dash around the courtyard. He would have them do five fast laps for the buyer's benefit.

"I don't know," Maleef replied absent mindedly as he tried to keep his eyes on the forms of the hurrying slave girls.

"These aren't fat peasant girls," Khalid continued. "They're a choice lot taken from the cities, Shanghai and Hong Kong mostly. Burnham's having them brought in."

"The Americans again," Maleef sighed. "Well, I may take one or two to see how they train. Is it true that their snatches release perfumed flowers when they come?" he asked laughing.

Khalid returned the laugh. "Don't be a bigot, Maleef. They're just like all the other women in the world. Burnham brought some down last month and we tried them out for a few days. They were excellent. Imagine the vast pool of sluts to pick from, all at the beck and call of the government apparatus. Most of them are athletes, shop girls or aspiring models or actresses. Burnham picks them out from a book that his contacts provide him. It's easy to collect them. Some pretense is made of some slanderous comment about the government and they're arrested, tried and convicted within a few days. Once they're sentenced, they can just disappear."

"Okay, okay," Maleef responded. "I'll take a look at them when they come in."

The girls had completed their fifth circuit of the courtyard and Khalid's men signaled them to reform in a line. They were huffing and puffing, their faces red and sweaty, their bodies slick with perspiration. Not too unlike what they would look like after a proper fucking. Maleef went down the small line of girls taking stock before they regained their breaths. This was the really hard part. Any one of them a man might give a week's pay just to fuck. But did they have that special something that he was looking for? One of the three blonds that he had in mind for his customer seemed peckish and tired. Her face was slack and her eyes were clouded. "No," he said curtly as he pointed at her. She rushed off to join her rejected sisters. He would keep the other two. That left four more to choose from the six remaining.

A short, brown haired girl seemed not to be able to recover from her travail. She was sobbing heavily. She was out. Five were left and he would choose four.

One of the remaining women had short, black hair cut into a pageboy. Her breasts were nice and round and she had pale, blue eyes. Her face gave off an animalistic contortion as she struggled to get her air back. She looked Italian or Greek. He would take her. That left two brunettes, a ponytailed blond and a girl with long, orange hair and pale, thin skin. She had a build like a model. Her lips were wide and her mouth broad. There was a little mole on the side of her small, right breast, but it gave her a certain charm. No man, despite what he might say, wanted to sleep with a perfect woman. It was like fucking a mannequin. They had to have some personality and the girl's mole was just the right touch. She was a mite thin, but would fill out. Her face and chest were flushed an attractive pink. He selected her.

The blond girl was in good physical shape, probably a runner in her former life. She had smooth, well toned skin with a certain aristocratic, well fed look. This type, born to privilege, was always hard to train. But the efforts were nearly always worth it. She would provide a definite elegance to some master's seraglio. And once she had dedicated herself to her new occupation and given up all hopes of rescue or escape, she would devote herself to her tasks with a competitive enthusiasm. He would take her.

The last two brunettes presented a problem. One had long, brown hair that descended down her back, strait and thin. Her nipples were dainty and sat atop tiny, smooth swirls. Her breasts were a tad small, but they were well formed and she carried them very well. Her face had a certain look of sorrow, as if it was bred deeply within her, somewhat mystical. Her hips were narrow and her sparse, curly brown pubic hair barely disguised a delicate, dainty crevasse that was made for the whip.

The other brunette was buxom and broad hipped. Her nipples were long and she had large, dark areolas. She was not heavy set by any means and her torso had an enticing curve to it. Her belly sloped down invitingly to a full, plump, already shaven pudendum. Her thick upper lips were parted as she panted woefully before him. Her large brown eyes were troubled and brimming with tears, evidencing just the right level of vulnerability.

Maleef hated this. He always set himself a definite number to limit himself at Khalid's, but the choices were always so hard. If he chose the big breasted girl, and who could go wrong with that, he would have the dark souled, delicate, whip ready slut on his mind for the next week. "Fuck it," he thought.

"Okay," he told Khalid. "I'll take them all."

Khalid clapped his hands happily and his men commenced reequipping the still recovering women with their gags. They gave out cries and moans as they were herded to Maleef's truck. It was originally a furniture delivery van but had been equipped to serve his training house's purposes. Two rows of narrow cages had been installed on each side, one above the other. There were twenty four cages in all, twelve on each side, six on each level. Five of the cages were already filled, one with the talented, cocksucking brunette he had decided on earlier and four from a previous stop.

Maleef's assistant and driver supervised the loading. The two back doors of the van were swung open and each girl was made to step up inside, one by one. They were, as a group, sobbing and moaning at their unknown fates. They had passed a test, but what would be their reward? The man had handled them cruelly and coldly, as if he were buying furniture or animals. Some of the girls had been at Khalid's for over a week, some just a few days. One of the blonds had been just shipped in this morning with Deidre. They were of varying nationalities, American, Greek, Dutch, and more. The orange haired girl was a Scot. She had been selected after an open call for actresses for a commercial shoot in London. But regardless of their origins, they now all faced a similar fate.

One by one the unhappy women were loaded in. There was a foot ladder that was used to install the girls on the upper levels. The prior occupants, gagged and bound within their little prisons, watched forlornly as their new mates were lodged next to or across from them. The cages were made from heavy gauged steel rods, crossed horizontally and vertically and there were tiny square openings too small for more than a finger to pass through. Each woman's hands were rebound behind her and she was then forced to back into the cage and into a sitting position. The floors of the cages were padded and had a stainless steel drain in the middle under the women's sexes so that their liquid wastes would be collected in little pots underneath them. It was a three hour ride back to Maleef's training house and it would be unrealistic to believe that they wouldn't have to pee before then. Their knees were raised high in front of them and their ankles tied wide apart to rings in the floor. The cages were so narrow so that their backs were pushed up against the wall of the truck. There was no room to turn around, rise up or to change position.

Maleef watched, smoking a cigarette, as the dismally unhappy young women he had selected were loaded. He had two more stops to make before heading home. As usual, it had taken longer to go through Khalid's stock than he had anticipated. Although he had room for more women, he doubted that he would fill the truck out. He rarely did. But if the other facilities had more girls that he could use, he would have room for them.

The assistant was about to swing shut the two tall doors to the truck when Maleef heard someone approach him from behind. It was one of Khalid's men. They all wore black t-shirts and black dungaree pants with heavy brown boots. He had the red headed girl from the luncheon in tow. A rope was around her neck and her hands were bound behind her. Her leather collar and bracelets had been removed and a shield gag like all the other women wore had been added. Maleef looked at her in surprise and then at Khalid.

"A gift," Khalid said, making a wide arc with his arm as if in presentation of the German slut.

Maleef was only mildly surprised. Khalid would get a premium for his purchases today and he could well afford to throw another girl in. The German girl shook her head and pulled back on the leash that Khalid's man was holding. Better the devil that you knew than the one that you didn't. Maleef took the rope from the man and dragged the tall, voluptuous girl towards him. "As soon as we get to your new home, you're going to get a beating," he told her in English. "You've got to learn better manners."

The girl moaned and continued her efforts to pull away. Maleef just handed the end of the rope to his assistant and the man soon had the girl sitting in a cage, ready for transport. He hopped off the back of the truck and slammed the doors shut leaving the unhappy women inside in total darkness.

"Thank you, Khalid," Maleef told the grinning, black bearded man. "As usual, I am ever grateful." The two men kissed and Maleef walked over to the passenger side of the truck. He climbed aboard and the engine started. A moment or two later, the van passed through the gate to Khalid's little fortress and was gone.

Khalid waited until the gate had been closed again and then nodded to one of his men. A few minutes later, a whistle blew and a stream of naked, bound and gagged young women came pouring out of the barracks and began a speedy, unhappy trek around the courtyard.

CHAPTER TWO
A GIRL PAYS THE PIPER

Human beings can get used to most anything. There is something about our will to survive that makes our minds accommodate to any situation, even the most dreadful and debilitating. It is doubtful that the human race could have survived without the ability to adjust to changing, unfortunate circumstance.

For Maddy, it was no different. She had been a ponygirl for about eight months now. At first, she had cried and miserated over the loss of her human rights. Spirited away to a strange land, deprived of speech and all voluntary attributes, used callously as a sexual toy, deprived even of the right to see her own face, to touch her own body, Maddy had lost almost all will to live. The fear of her trainer's ever ready lash and the barest hope that someday, somehow, she would be rescued, kept her going. She survived by living day to day, blocking her memories of who she once was, accepting her fate.

There were two things that had really provided impetus to put aside her piteous ruminations over her lost life. One was the experience of her first victory as a ponygirl. Her training had been harsh and cruel. She had suffered many blows of the whip, both as an encouragement to greater effort and as a punishment for less than acceptable results. But the first time that she had crossed the finish line ahead of her competitor, been rewarded by a celebratory victory lap around the track, a thrill had run through her. After that, she had pledged to herself to devote her entire being to achieving victory. Now, she yearned to hear the yelling and screaming of her ponygirl name, "*Molnya, Molnya, Molnya*" by the excited crowd as she entered the winner's circle. She welcomed her driver's harsh lash on her back and rear during their rigorous training sessions, impelling her to effort beyond which would otherwise have been possible. At the end of the spring season, it had brought her a championship in her division, the 1500 meter sulky, a one pony cart. The men had affixed a golden medal to her ponygirl collar that she wore proudly. Although she had seen it only once, when her driver presented it to her before he attached it to the front ring of her collar beyond her view, she could feel it dangling there as she walked or ran and could see as others, men and other ponygirls as well, had their eyes drawn to it. It had been taken away at the beginning of this, the fall racing season, by her driver as a reminder that she could not rest on her laurels and must earn her right to be considered a ponygirl champion all over again.

The second thing that assuaged her dismal unhappiness at being transformed into a voiceless, confined beast was her original trainer. He was a cruel, callous man with shoulder length, ink black hair, a scar across his right cheek, tall and muscular. It was he who first taught her how to run in her shin high ponygirl boots, her neck confined by the wide, chin uplifting, leather covered, stiff, ponygirl collar, her hands bound behind her. It was he who had first applied the since then ever present, confining and dehumanizing, Neoprene ponygirl hood that covered her head and face down to below her chin, exposing only her lips and the edges of her nostrils. The holes for her eyes were just tiny, dime sized dots, limiting her vision to just what was absolutely necessary for a ponygirl to see.

Somehow, the man had developed a special bond with her. She had felt it too, a response to the only man who had shown her human feelings since her kidnapping. At first, once he had realized the thrall that she had unwittingly cast over him, he had reacted cruelly and with vengeance. He had beaten her severely and ensured that she received extra abuse from the other trainers and the grooms of the ponygirl barn. But after the spring season, he had somehow come to terms with his affection for her and had treated her kindly. He often came down to her stall in the pony barn during the interregnum between seasons, 'ponygirl summer', as they referred to it, and used her, sometimes tenderly, sometimes forcefully, but always with passion. On a few occasions, he had taken her out and had her pull him on a cart along the bucolic paths and trails that surrounded the estate. Finding a shady glade, he had unhooked her from her traces and caressed and stroked her with his thick, hard cock to pleasure in the grass. She loved the feel of him in her mouth and thrilled to bring him to pleasure that way, kneeling between his thighs, her hands bound behind her, with only her lips and tongue to give him adoration.

Maddy did not know his name and she had not seen him since she had been handed over to the devilish dwarf who was her driver. Since the sulky was a one pony cart, and speed was of the essence, the lighter the driver, the lighter the load that she had to pull. Therefore, the role of driver was ideally suited to these diminutive men and most of the sulkies were driven by either dwarves, when they could be recruited, or by the slimmest and lightest men that could be found. The fact that her driver was a dwarf did not mitigate his cruelty nor his determination and ability to rule her with an iron fist.

It was an inviolable rule that once a ponygirl had been delivered to her driver for the racing season, she was no longer available for the routine, casual sexual use that was the norm back in the pony barn. Her driver controlled everything about her, when she ate, when she slept, when she fucked and when she was permitted to orgasm. The last was the real hardship since, as a ponygirl, fucking and running were the only two pleasures open to her. Proper ponygirl handling dictated that the dehumanized creatures be subjected to a steady diet of pain and sexual excitement. The concept was that, as animals, their focus was to be entirely on their bodies and not their minds. And so a ponygirl, left alone in her tiny, enclosed stall for many hours a day, standing with her waist jammed up against a rail, her nose ring attached to a chain that led to the empty wall in front of her, her ankles locked widely apart, would find her mind, eventually, turning from thoughts of her dismal plight to reminiscences about her recent use and anticipation of her next opportunity for a body wrenching, mind numbing orgasm. That, and on how to avoid her trainer's whip.

The events of this evening had cast a pall over the tall, big breasted ponygirl. Jerzi, her driver, had left the camp to join with some of his fellow drivers in some merriment at their encampment. Tomorrow was a racing day and they were on their home estate, that belonging to the Russian gangster Axmail Grobgy. The season was seven weeks old and almost over. Maddy was a shoo-in to qualify for the Fall Championship Tournament in two weeks. And the other estate teams had done well. The estate had won the overall in the spring and it was very probable that they could repeat this fall. The overall championship was based on points, so much awarded for each race won and for final placement in the Fall Tournament. The yearlings, a two pony team made up of ponies new to their bits, had done well. The phaetons and the chaises, both four pony carts, one set for speed, the other for endurance, carrying both a driver and a passenger at regulated, minimum weights, were both in the championship, although they would probably not win, as was the stylish, six pony cabriolet if it won tomorrow's race. *Molnya*, 'Lightning' in Russian, was a favorite to champion as was the pony who now ran the 1500 meter, the race that Lightning ran last season. For reasons known only to her masters, Lightning had been moved up to the 3000 meter, a struggle at first, but a race that her strength and speed was well suited for.

Lightning had been left standing at the rear of her traveling trailer, the back of her collar connected by a short chain to a ring about six feet high, preventing her from crouching or kneeling or to move more than a few inches in any direction. It was not uncommon for the ponygirls to be left in a display position such as this so that passers by might admire them. Her driver's servant, a skinny, short, black haired, Rumanian slave girl, had been left kneeling inside the camp, gagged, her wrists and ankles bound to each other, to await the return of her master from his revelries. She was the one who undertook the day to day maintenance of the ponygirl, shaving her head and pudenda each day, massaging her aching muscles after a race or workout, feeding and cleaning her. She would also use her mouth or hands to drive the ponygirl near to a pleasurable orgasm several times a day, but not completion. For it was Jerzi's firm method to deny his charge orgasmic delight unless as a reward for a successful race or other accomplishment. He deemed it better that the animal be yearning for the denied release of her sexual energies at the commencement of each race, a strategy that seemed to serve him well since he had, in the past, driven several ponygirl champions. Needless to say, for an animal used to achieving orgasm many times a day, it was an excruciating torment to be caressed and stroked to intense sexual passion every few hours by the little, black haired, slave girl without achievement.

But tomorrow was a racing day and Lightning's mind was drifting over the probability that she would receive a round fucking by her driver when the race was over. At other times, he denied her the benefits of his cock except to use her mouth to empty his spewm in after his slave girl had stoked his fires. But even then, Lightning was denied the thrill of his pulsing throbbing rod between her lips, but instead, was forced to hold her obediently yawning lips wide open while he stroked his thick prick and pumped his load upon her tongue, giving her the product of his pleasure but not the pleasure itself.

Tomorrow would be different. Tomorrow, she would do everything in her power to claim the garland of flowers draped around the neck of the victorious ponygirls and, after she was brought back to the camp, enjoy the full pleasures of her master's rampant prick.

It was dark, the ponies had all been fed, and the trail between the individual encampments was lit only by the glow of the campfires amidst them. Even the moon had fled. Lightning could hear the sounds of the men singing one of their drinking songs a few campsites over. The merry, deep, male voices were almost comforting, a welcome familiarity. It meant that her master would probably return in a good mood and not whip her before he retired to fuck his little, black haired, slave girl.

The pony was not surprised to hear people walking up the narrow pathway between the trailers. As they approached, she realized that they were not regular denizens of the encampment. First of all, one of them was a young woman. Not that it was unusual to see women scurrying along the hard packed dirt road. All of the drivers had their little slave girls to run their errands and she would frequently see the naked, young girls hustling to their destinations wearing a mouth confining shield across their faces and, often, with their hands bound behind them by their slave bracelets, their burdens slung around their necks or across their shoulders.

This woman, however, was fully dressed. She was wearing a long, white dress with ruffles that ran around the skirt and a full bodice with puffed up, short sleeves. In one hand, she carried a small bouquet of little flowers. Her other hand was enclosed around the hand of her partner, a slender youth dressed in a sports jacket over a white shirt and dark pants. As they approached closer, Lightning could see that he was clean shaven and had short, well trimmed hair. He looked to be in his mid-twenties. The girl was somewhat younger, maybe 20 or so, had a slender, shapely figure and a pretty face.

Lightning had often seen women at the races that she had run. It seemed that they were inured to the cruel fates of the ponies and enjoyed the spectacle of the naked, hooded, former women trotting around the track at full speed, breasts akimbo, whips cracking at their backs. At the opening of the season, it was traditional for the estate owner to have a huge party at which the ponygirls that were to race the next day would be displayed for the perusal of his guests. Lightning had, at first, resented the eyes of the pretty, well dressed women scouring her naked flesh, her bonds, her featureless face. She had gotten used to it by now and it rarely brought back those feelings of unfairness and injustice at her fate that it once had.

The sight of these two young people approaching her filled her with foreboding and distress. It was one thing to be displayed naked on the ponygirl track before a thousand or two anonymous people, or to be part of a display of ponygirls, one among many, on a ceremonial occasion. But these two 'civilians', as it were, had intruded into the closed and hermetic atmosphere of the ponygirl camp. The sight of the pretty girl holding hands with her presumptive boyfriend brought back painful memories and a yearning for the warmth of human relations.

When they came close to Lightning, she could see that the young man was excited. He pulled his girlfriend closer so that they could get a better look at the naked ponygirl. The light from the nearby campfire flickered on their youthful, happy faces as they stood in front of her. The boy said something to the girl in Russian and she giggled. The ponygirl heard her name, '*Molnya*', mentioned. She backed away when the boy reached out his hand to her breasts but was prevented from avoiding his touch by the trailer behind her.

"See," the boy said to the girl in Russian, "I told you, it's Lightning!" He, like many others, followed the ponygirl racing circuit closely and had come to the Grobgy estate to watch the races the next day. The ponygirl camp lay about a half mile away from the grandstand and the track. On the other side of the track was a large field where aficionados of the sport could camp out prefatory to the next day's races. Since the estates were somewhat remote from the main population center of the country, it was often the only way that most people could get to see the races. It was a seven hour drive from Dlitski to the Grobgy estate. Most people would make a vacation of it, following a team from estate to estate to catch three or four races in a seven day period. The boy and his girl had driven up today and planned to return to the capital tomorrow after the race. He could not resist the urge to see the ponygirls up close and had bribed a guard to let them into the encampment. He had, though, been warned to look but not touch.

Lightning felt the boy's hand seize her breast and give it a squeeze. She gave out a whine of disapproval and tried to shake it off, but it made him grasp it all the more firmly. As a ponygirl, Lightning was trained to unquestioning obedience and she was not sure how far that this extended to these clear interlopers. It was better to be safe than sorry. A single kick from her strong, booted foot would send the boy howling away with pain, but she didn't dare risk the severe beating such an act would bring her.

"Don't, Sergei," the girl protested. "You heard what the guard said."

"Oh, come on, Zhanna, don't be a scaredy cat. No one's looking." The boy released the girl's hand and seized Lightning's other breast. "They're so soft and full," he said. He leaned over and took one of the ponygirl's nipples in his mouth and suckled it gently. "Mmmmmmmmmm," he moaned. He turned to his girlfriend and smiled. "It's delicious."

Zhanna looked at Sergei with disdain. "Come on Sergei," she said, "you shouldn't be doing that."

"Why not," Sergei replied, his hands still massaging the unhappy ponygirl's breasts.

"Because it's not right, that why," Zhanna replied.

"Oh, get off it, Zhanna! She just a ponygirl."

"She's a woman, Sergei, no matter what the men have done to her."

"You're not going to start that again, are you?" the boy returned to her, annoyed. "Then why did you agree to come up here with me?"

"To see what it would be like, that's all," Zhanna insisted.

"Well, you won't know what it's really like until you touch her, Zhanna. Here, take a feel of her tits. They're marvelous."

"I'm not in the habit of touching other women's breasts, Sergei."

"But that's just it, Zhanna. She's not a woman. Not anymore. Just look at how her body's reacting. She's hot already. She's just waiting to be fucked."

Through the tiny holes in her hood, Lightning could see the boy's contagious excitement spread across the young girl's face. She licked her pretty lips and reached out her small hand. Lightning could not understand their conversation, but she knew that they were discussing her and their low conspiratorial voices were a good indication that they had no right to touch her. Obedience was deeply ingrained in her psyche by now and she would have no more thought of resisting them than of resisting a master.

The boy let his hand off of one of Lightning's breasts so that the girl could touch it. "Oooooooouuuu!" she sighed as her soft, light fingers made contact with Lightning's firm, heavy mound. "It feels so nice," she whispered to the boy. Lightning could feel the girl's pretty dress as it brushed up against her belly and thighs. The girl's pleasant, innocent face was inches away from hers. Her flesh tingled where the young girl had touched her and she felt her juices release down below.

"I told you, Zhanna," Sergei said. The boy slid his free hand down over Lightning's tight belly and thrust it between her thighs. Lightning was trained to immediate response to sexual stimulation, no matter from whom, and when the boy discovered her moistness he whispered excitedly to his girlfriend, "She's already wet, Zhanna! You've got to feel this!"

The girl, her own excitement growing, joined Sergei's hand between the ponygirl's thighs.

"Oh my gosh," she said, astounded at the pony's quick reaction.

"See, I told you. She's just an animal now. She just looks like a woman. What woman would get wet at the drop of a hat like that?"

Lightning was trying to resist the effects of her stimulation by the young couple, having little success. As the girl's fingers joined the boy's at her loins, she gave a little moan from behind her gagged lips. The girl looked up at her with a new appreciation of her status. She stepped back and took a long look at her body lit only by the faint, flickering light of a nearby campfire. She saw her name, "*Molnya*", stenciled in large, blue letters across her chest, the tattoo of the emblem of her estate, the fierce, snarling, yellow wolf, emblazoned on her lower belly, just above her hairless sex. She looked at her large, firm, naked breasts and her solid, muscular thighs. But most of all, she looked at the smooth, featureless face covered by the taut, blue hood. In the dark, she could not even peer into the tiny little holes of the hood to see if there was a person in there. There was a large, shiny, gold colored ring in the pony's nose, clearly not something any woman would have. Her lips were sealed by the broad, leather shield that covered the lower half of her face. And she had no use of her arms. "Is this a woman?" she asked herself. She began to doubt it. Maybe she once was, but she was something else now. The hand that was lodged in Lightning's sex brushed against the medallions that were affixed to her love lips, at the bottom near her perineum, medallions that carried the crest and name of her current owner, Axmail Grobgy. "Oh," the startled girl cried. She had not realized. If further proof of her dehumanized state was needed, this was it.

"I want to fuck her," Sergei told the girl conspire-atorially, his voice carrying the evidence of his growing lust. His fingers were actively rubbing Lightning's distended, stiffened clit and the pony squirmed and whined in automatic response.

"I don't know...." the girl murmured. She had become fascinated by the body of the former human beast before her. She leaned forward, unable to resist, and took one of Lightning's nipples in her mouth, sucking on it gently. The soft, pleasant lips of the girl pulling on her teat in combination with the continued stimulation of her loins caused Lightning to moan. Her knees became weak and her body shuddered.

"Come on," the boy challenged. "You can rub her tits while I fuck her from behind. We'll never get this chance again."

When the girl's lips released Lightning's teat her face was aglow with passion. She would never let her boyfriend fuck another girl in front of her, nor at any other time either. But this was different. It was so hot! And it was something that would spice up their sex life for a long time to come. Never mind what she would tell her girlfriends. And this was *Molnya*, the great sulky pony! How great was that? Besides, what difference would it make to the animal? She heard that ponygirls were fucked ten times a day at least. "Okay," she whispered lustfully to Sergei.

Lightning shook her head in protest when the boy reached behind her and unhooked the chain that led to her collar. Her wrists pulled futilely at her bonds and her hands writhed. "This shouldn't be happening!" she thought desperately. "Please don't so this, please!" her mind cried out. The outside world was intruding on the special place she had created for herself. She was resigned to being a ponygirl as long as the idea that there was no alternative was firmly fixed in her psyche. But this boy and this girl had broken that barrier. Just as much as they could pull her off into the bushes and abuse her, they could set her free. And the girl! Didn't she realize what it must be like to lose your freedom this way? Didn't she have any consideration for her as a living, breathing, feeling woman? Or did the disguise that she wore, her ponygirl raiment, really take all of that away from her?

Lightning made a move to shy away from the young couple once her chain was unhooked, but the boy took hold of the ring in her nose and tugged at it harshly. She gave a moan of unhappiness as he led her off. Within two steps away from the trailer they were in almost complete darkness. The boy moved quickly into the adjoining woods, Lightning stumbling unhappily after him. She could hear the giggles of the girl as they moved further and further away from the encampment. When they reached a small clearing, the boy pulled downwards on her nose ring until Lightning fell to her knees.

The boy took a position behind her and the girl in front. Her body shuddered as he ran his soft hands over her rear globes and her curvaceous hips. She was kneeling over, her legs spread, having assumed automatically the position that she had assumed so many times before in anticipation of her use. The girl leaned down and took possession of her breasts, kneading and massaging them gently, pulling lightly on her stiffened nipples. Lightning's covered face was buried in the girl's shoulder and she could smell her delicate perfume. Her lust was growing as the boy began to rub the moistened, engorged love lips between her thighs.

It had been two days since she had had a cock inside her and the torments that the black haired girl had visited upon her, urging on her passions, but not satisfying them, had created a deep pool of need within her. She felt the boy's hands leave and sensed him freeing his cock from his pants behind her. He drew his hardened piece along the length of her slit, bringing on a deep, lust filled moan from the ponygirl. She felt the tip of his rock hard meat enter her and then slide its way down the length of her trembling canal and she groaned with pleasure.

While the girl stimulated her hot breasts, the boy sawed his stiff pole along her electrified shaft. All reservations about what was happening dissolved as Lightning reveled in the feel of a prick coursing along her feverish canal. She moaned again as his thighs slapped against hers, his flat belly resting against her proffered, round rear globes. She could hear him panting and straining at his task as he jammed his cock back and forth rapidly. He had, of course, little concern for her pleasure, but that was of no consequence; few of the masters did. She took her pleasure how and when she could find it and the boy's pistoning cock drove her lusts higher and higher. Her orgasm preceded his by mere seconds. Her body shuddered and her pussy erupted in intense, fierce contractions around his pole. In her fevered lust, she heard the boy groan.

The girl squealed with pleasure as she took in the shadowy vision of her boyfriend mounting and fucking the ponygirl in the dim light. The pony's full, spongy breasts were hot in her hands as she caressed them and her nipples made little points in her soft palms. She thought of Sergei's cock and how she would lustfully accept it in her own hot quim later this very night, her mind filled with the excitement of this moment. When she heard him coming and felt the body of the ponygirl tense and shake with her own orgasm, she nearly came herself right then and there.

Her attention was focused keenly on the tableau before her. It shifted, though, when she heard a dull thud. Her boyfriend groaned and slid off of the ponygirl. Hard, strong hands gripped her arms and lifted her up. She looked around and saw a group of coarse, muscular men surrounding them and she screamed.

Jerzi had been beside himself when he saw that the ponygirl was gone. He saw in the dirt a small clump of flowers that someone had dropped. He ran quickly to the nearest campsite and alerted the other men, sending one of them to advise the pony's owner, Axmail Grobgy. Since the one side of the road was lined with campsites, there was only one way that the thieves could have gone. The group of men came upon the fornicating trio just as the ponygirl and the boy had been noisily reaching their climax, masking the sound of their approach. Jerzi picked up a large log from the ground and, advancing on them quietly, smacked the boy across his head just at the peak of his delight.

Zhanna continued to scream and attempted to struggle as the strong hands threw her to the ground. She felt her arms yanked behind her back and tied off by a leather strap. Someone pulled her to her feet and a fist struck her in her belly, pushing out all of her air and silencing her in mid scream.

Lightning began to sob uncontrollably. She had no idea what was happening, only that she had been treated like one of the lowest forms of animals on earth. "Why? Why? Why?" she thought miserably as her sorrow poured out of her. "Why am I here? What have these men done to me?"

The men who had come to rescue her were holding bright torches and the little glen in which she knelt danced with light and shadow. She felt a hand under her chin and a leash clipped to her collar. She was pulled to her feet and led back to the camp.

The men dragged the unconscious body of the boy and the gasping, moaning body of the girl into the camp area. The boy was quickly bound hand and foot and the girl's already bound wrists were tied off to her ankles. Someone had retrieved a gag from the trailer and it was shoved into her gasping mouth and buckled behind her head as she tried desperately to regain her air.

Jerzi was beside himself with anger. He stepped over to the boy, who was gradually returning to consciousness, and gave him a mighty kick in the ribs with his boot, causing the boy to groan with pain. When the groan subsided to a moan, he kicked him again. He walked over to the girl who was staring wide eyed at him and whining piteously and gave her a vicious slap across the face. She emitted a muffled shriek from behind her gag and he slapped her again.

Only then did he turn to the distraught, sobbing ponygirl. Something had snapped in her and had she not been supported by the strong arms of a couple of the other drivers, she would have fallen to the ground. He looked her body over carefully, searching for signs of physical injury. Seeing none, he signaled the men to release her and she sank to her knees.

The campsite was crowded with drivers and groomers incensed at the actions of the irresponsible young couple. A bottle was passed around easing somewhat their anger, but fueling their thoughts of revenge. Nothing would be done until Grobgy arrived, although everyone knew that the consequences for the foolish young man and the pretty young woman would be grim. It was about the worst thing that you could do to abscond with a ponygirl, even if it was only to have a little fun with her. Even its owner didn't have the right, without the consent of the driver, to use one during the racing season. The ponygirls were kept in a state of highly focused control and any interference could disturb the delicate balance of their training. Races could be lost, careers ruined. Men had been killed for much less.

Jerzi paced up and down the small encampment barely able to contain himself. He stepped up to the crying, moaning girl and, reaching for the bodice of the dress, tore it open down to her waist and pulled its sleeves down her arms, revealing her delicate, plump globes encased in a lacy, white bra. She screeched as she felt herself bared. The incensed driver pulled out a knife and sliced the bra open, letting the soft, round orbs fall free.

Zhanna was beside herself with fright. She realized that she was in a lot of trouble, that something was going to happen that she would not be able to bear. Why had they done it, she though miserably. It was stupid and now they faced the consequences. When her breasts were bared before all of the angry men, she realized that she would probably have to pay for her crime with her body and she gave a disheartened, piteous moan. The roaring fire in the middle of the encampment made the faces of the men all grotesque and demonic, especially the contorted, hate filled face of the little man who had exposed her breasts. She feared him most of all.

The dwarfish ponygirl driver walked to the trailer and returned with a long, thin, leather lash. He signaled one of the other men to grab the girl. The man took hold of her long, brown hair and pulled her up so that her torso was extended. Her ample breasts jutted out enticingly. Jerzi reared his hand back and laid the cruel lash across the pretty girl's defenseless mounds.

The poor girl howled when she felt the leather kiss her delicate orbs. "Oh god! Oh god! Oh god!" she cried out in her mind as the pain shot through her. It was like someone had lit a line of fire across her breasts. "…..ease …on't! ….ease …on't!" she tried to cry through the stifling leather that filled her mouth. But the whip came down again, like a jagged razor tearing into her flesh. "Ooouuuuuuuuuuuu!

Ouuuuuuuuuuuuuu!" she cried out. Her scalp ached where the man held her hair behind her as she tried to twist her body to avoid the blows. Her hands pulled desperately at her bonds and her knees ground into the hard dirt below her.

Jerzi wasn't finished. He laid the lash again across her pale, white orbs, aiming carefully for her tender nipples and scored spot on. The girl screeched and her body contorted as she absorbed the blow. Tears were flowing like a river down her pretty face.

It was then that Grobgy appeared. The circle of men became silent as he breached it and even Jerzi stopped to give him his attention.

Axmail Grobgy was a murderous gangster. His men ran all kinds of contraband in and out of the new Russia, extorted millions from legitimate businessmen, ran gambling and prostitution in Moscow and Petersburg. He had extended his nefarious reach into the Ukraine as well. Hundreds of men had lost their lives at his command. He possessed a vast estate here in Kalikastan, housing more than two dozen ponygirls and thirty or more slave girls. He was a former KGB sergeant who, knowing where the bodies were buried, and being a ruthless, conscienceless kind of fellow, prospered quickly when the old Soviet Union had collapsed. Although technically under indictment back in Russia, his criminal power had been left undiminished. You didn't want to fuck with Axmail Grobgy.

And you didn't want to fuck either with the dark, broad shouldered, black haired man who appeared next to him. Anton Drabik was Grobgy's chief killer. Just his presence at the ad hoc circle of concerned drivers and trainers was enough for some of the energy to seep out of the crowd. Drabik doubled as a ponygirl trainer, one of the best, and it was the young man and woman's unfortunate circumstance that they had been fooling around with his favorite, the one who had stolen his soul. Drabik was Lightning's trainer and he was well prepared to make anyone who had done ill to her pay with their lives.

The tall, heavyset gang leader, Grobgy, took stock of the situation. It was related to him how the couple had been found and what they had been up to. He looked over at the young man, who had been dragged to his knees. He was moaning from his broken ribs and had a look of desperate fear on his face.

"Who is he?" Grobgy asked the crowd. It would not be unheard of for another estate to try and sabotage a competitor's ponygirl, although from the look of the sallow youth, Grobgy doubted that this was the case. The men in the crowd shrugged. Exasperated, Grobgy yelled out, "Well, does he have a wallet?"

One of the men who was standing behind the youth reached into his back pants pocket and pulled out a wad of leather. He respectfully and gingerly approached the crime lord and handed it to him. The boy, seeing his wallet handed to the fearsome looking man called out to him. "Please, please, we didn't mean any harm! I'm sorry! Please don't hurt us!"

Grobgy looked over at the boy disdainfully. He had heard plenty of men plead for their lives and it sickened him. He took two deliberate steps over to the boy, whose hands were confined behind his back, and unleashed his big right fist against the side of his face. There was a loud cracking sound as the boy's jaw broke. He fell to his side crying and blubbering from the pain. He was quickly lifted back to his knees.

The angry gangster looked rapidly through the wallet. If this kid was somebody's nephew or son, he would have to bring the case before the Commission. He pulled out some cash and threw it to the ground. There was an identity card. He did not recognize the last name. The boy was nobody. He looked into the boy's frightened eyes and tossed the identity card and the wallet and the rest of its contents onto the fire. The boy watched, horrified, realizing that this act spelled his doom.

"Oh, no, please! Please!" the boy yelled. His voice was gargled and muffled as a result of the swelling that had arisen already on the side of his formerly handsome face. Grobgy put his hand on the pistol that was holstered on his waist. The boy moaned as he saw the strong, callous hand make its motion.

"No!" Jerzi called out. "He's mine!" The dwarf had a large, broad bladed knife in his hand. The gang leader recognized immediately the justice of the little man's claim. It was his livelihood the boy had fucked with. For the racing season, the ponygirl was his. Grobgy indicated his concession to the smaller man's superior rights.

The young man watched in terror as the diminutive, evil looking man approached him. His yelling had been reduced to a piteous whine. "Please don't kill me, please," he squeaked. The dwarf showed the young man his shiny, sharp blade and then crossed behind him. He took hold of a tuft of hair at the back of his head and, quickly and efficiently, before the boy could even emit another piteous plea for mercy, dragged the knife deeply across his exposed throat.

There was a surge of blood, some of it darting out into middle of the small encirclement of approving men, the rest flowing down his clean, white shirt. The foolish, young man gurgled and coughed and then fell to the ground face down as Jerzi gave his body a little shove. He writhed slightly and his body jerked twice and then he was still.

Zhanna screamed in dismay when she saw her boyfriend's life blood pour out of him. She had never seen a man killed before. She watched the life escape from her lover's body, forlornly knowing full well that his death bode evil for her too. Her body convulsed as she sobbed, her eyes spread open wide in terror, her hands desperately seeking release from their cruel confinement behind her.

Grobgy looked around at the circle of men. "Okay, you can go now," he shouted at them in his deep, commanding voice. "Tend to your stock and go to bed. It's all over."

But it wasn't over, all the men knew that. There was still the fate of the pretty, young girl to be decided. Her delicious breasts, marred by three, angry, red stripes, bounced enticingly as she cried and wailed in her bonds. They knew that her fate would not be as simple as a short, intense sensation of pain across her throat and then darkness. Her body was too alluring, her breasts too firm and enticing for that. But, whatever Grobgy had in mind for her, he had spoken and, as much as they wanted to enjoy the show, they reluctantly took heed of his command and began to sidle back to their camps.

Several of Grobgy's security men had come with him and they stood behind him, Kalashnikov rifles dangling over their shoulders. "Get this body out of here," Grobgy ordered them. Two of the men moved forward on command and, taking the dead youth by his ankles, dragged him from the circle of light. Grobgy turned to look at the girl. Her muffled sobs had faded and she returned his gaze forlornly. He stepped up and crouched down in front of her.

"So, you wanted to see what a ponygirl was like, eh?" he asked her tauntingly. He took hold of her hair and pointed her head at the kneeling, still gently sobbing ponygirl. "Did you get a good enough look?" Grobgy asked the frightened, young woman. He ran his hand over her lacerated breasts, pinching her nipples harshly as he went, causing the girl to moan with pain.

"Maybe you didn't get a good enough look? Maybe you'd like to see what it's like to be a ponygirl first hand, eh?"

The girl shook her head frantically as much as Grobgy's steel like grip on her head allowed.

"Oh, I think that you'll find that it's lots of fun. I can always use another pretty, little ponygirl. Did you get a good look at your face this morning when you put on your makeup? It's the last time that you'll ever see it. Did you use your hands to fondle my ponygirl's pretty breasts or her delightful snatch? That's the last time that you'll ever use them. Do you have a name? Forget it. We'll give you a new one."

Grobgy continued to maul the girl's sensitive, bruised breasts as he taunted her. Her mind screamed with denial of her prospective fate. She didn't want to become a ponygirl. She would rather that they killed her. She thought of her friends and family back in the capital. She would never see them again, nor they her, unless they happened to watch her as she paraded down the race track at the head of some cart, naked and bound for all to see.

They probably wouldn't even know it was her, she thought miserably.

The unreality of what was happening struck the girl and she began to sob again. She wanted to beg and plead to be set free, tell the man that she was sorry. She rued her mistake in assuming that the ponygirl had no feelings and the dissolution of her initial inclination to insist that Sergei leave the poor, unfortunate female alone. Why had she come here? She had been curious about the stories told about the specially imbonded former women, had wanted to see for herself if what people said was true. But now she was caught up in an inescapable trap. She was in these cruel men's power and there was no one to help her. She moaned with pain as the fearsome looking man twisted her nipples again cruelly.

Grobgy had had enough of tormenting the stupid girl. "Get a ponygirl hood and some shears," he commanded. "And a razor."

The girl whined deeply as she heard the command. She struggled fiercely as the men dragged her to the center of the little circle. One of the men grabbed her around the neck with his strong arm as another removed her gag. Her voice was free for maybe the last time in her life. Her hands and feet twisted frantically in her bonds. She had one last chance to beg the men not to condemn her to a life of brutality and pain. "Pleeeeeease don't!" she yelled at the top of her lungs. "Please! Please! Please! I'll do any...."

One of the men had torn off a part of her dress and rolled it into a ball. He stuffed it into her distended mouth in the middle of her plea and silenced her. She moaned and cried in dismal frustration.

Grobgy took a seat next to the dwarfish driver as his men saw to the soon to be dehumanized young girl. The small man's slave girl, Natasha, had brought out some glasses and more chairs and then set a little table down in front of them. Drabik and two of the security men sat down in them. She poured them each a glass of vodka which they all took down in one gulp. Lightning was kneeling next to Grobgy, still sobbing softly. She had watched as they murdered the boy and as her owner mocked and teased the helpless girl. She didn't want this. As far as she was concerned, they could have just let the young couple go. What had they done to her that dozens of men hadn't done before? Why did there have to be more misery and unhappiness? Why didn't they just let her crawl onto her pallet under the trailer and go to sleep?

Grobgy heard the ponygirl's low sobs and ran his hand over her smooth, hooded head in a gesture of comfort. "There, there, little *Molnya*," he called to her softly. "Don't worry, everything will be all right."

Lightning could not understand the words, but she received the gentle tone of the cruel man. She had clamped her eyes shut when she had seen the boy's throat slit like a ripe tomato and she opened them as she felt the soothing caress of her head and the warm voice. When she did, she saw for the first time the figure of her trainer looking over at her. The bright light of the fire and her tiny view on the world from her confining hood had prevented her from seeing him until now. He had anger in his eyes as he watched her owner lay his hand on her. Her heart yearned for his touch. She wanted to call out to him, to fall into his arms, to feel his body crushing hers as he drove his manhood deep within her. But there might as well as have been a hundred miles between them rather than a mere ten feet.

His angry look made her stomach sink. Was he angry at her? What had she done? Her heart trembled as considered that he might abandon her. What would she do then?

But it was not Lightning that Drabik cast his hate filled eyes at. It was Grobgy. For too long had he chafed under the leadership of the coarse former KGB sergeant. Drabik had been a colonel in the Red Army when the Soviet Union bust all to hell and he had been out of a job. His stint as a battalion commander in Afghanistan had taught him to be a cruel, cold killer and that was the only skill that he had when he was released 'for economic reasons' from his command. He had sought employment in the underworld and his cool, practiced, killer's hand stood him in good stead. He had been working for Grobgy now for over ten years. But the time had come to put the old bastard away. He had his plans and they were almost ripe. He would strike right after the Fall Tournament was over. His men were in place and he had received approval from the National Commission to make his move. Grobgy had been slipping and everyone agreed that it was time for him to go.

As he watched the gang leader's hand slide over Lightning's encapsulated head, Drabik seethed. It was bad enough that the ponygirl who had bewitched him was in the hands of the cruel dwarf for the next few weeks, but to watch Grobgy lay his hands on her, reaffirming his property claim to her was too much. If Grobgy didn't have his gunmen with him he might just do him right now, to hell with the consequences. But the men were there and he was sure that, unless he was able to get them all, he would end up dead himself. No, patience was the watchword. Patience, patience, patience, just like laying an ambush for those devilish so called freedom fighters back in Afghanistan. He would wait. He would burn, but he would wait.

The men in the middle of the camp were busy shearing off the unfortunate young girl's locks. They had first confined a skein of her long, straight, reddish brown hair in a ponytail and then commenced lopping everything else off. The girl squealed and writhed, uttering muffled, indecipherable pleas for mercy as she felt her growth being sliced away. But one of the men still held her neck firmly in the crux of his arm and she was unable to avoid the relentlessly snipping, steel shears as they denuded her head.

The men didn't bother to shave her cranium free of all of her stubble. That could be done later or tomorrow in the pony barn. It was enough that the ponygirl hood be able to lie flat and smooth over her head. While the man held her neck still, the smooth, blue neoprene hood was stretched over the top of her head and then, once her ponytail had been threaded through the little hole in the back, pulled down covering her face. It took a second to arrange the mouthhole over her lips and adjust the openings for her nostrils, nostrils that tomorrow would be adorned with a thick, golden ring. Just like all the other ponygirls had.

Zhanna, or the girl that would soon cease to be her, cried as her vision was reduced to the two little holes in the hood. The rag that had been thrust into her mouth was pulled out and the thick, mouth filling leather prong was again forced between her lips. The straps to the gag were pulled tightly behind her head and her lower face was covered with the leather shield that adorned the gag, right down to her chin.

The men released the moaning, crying girl. For all practical purposes, her conversion from a young, delightful, pretty, young girl to a beast had been complete. The essential part of her humanity, her face, had been permanently obscured, but for the brief periods that the hood would be removed for the cleaning of her face and head and for the daily removal of the stubble which would grow on her scalp. Her face would always be turned away from her handlers when that was done, for it was an ironclad rule never to look at a ponygirl's face. She would certainly never see it again, as her stall in the pony barn would not come equipped with a vanity mirror.

The men took a moment to appreciate their handiwork. The pony's breasts shimmered and swayed as she bemoaned her fate. Her small nipples were rigid from fear. The sole skein of hair that had been left on her head flowed through a hole in the rear of her smooth, blue hood and dangled down onto her back. She was still adorned with the tattered remnants of her lovely, ruffled, white dress and she would need other accouterments of her new status to complete the picture, but she was a ponygirl now all right. It was just like she had been one all along and didn't know it. All it took was a foolish misstep to complete her destiny. Her fate had called her all the way from the capital to this moment. Now she could begin her real life, the one before being just a prelude to the preordained role she had now assumed.

While the girl continued to cry, the men cut away the rest of her now incongruous clothing. They snipped away the sleeves of her pretty white dress and then, after rending it down the rest of the way from her waist, tore it from her. Her severed bra hung from her shoulders and that too was soon gone, cast into the fire which blazed in the middle of the encampment along with the rag that had been her dress. She had been wearing dainty, little white socks and black, low heeled shoes. They joined the conflagration. All that was left was a cute pair of lacy, white panties, the last that she would ever wear. Two snips at each gusset and they too were gone.

One of Drabik's men had run off to the tack room on the other side of the estate and he returned to see the keening, new ponygirl kneeling forlornly amidst the small group of admiring men. The vodka had passed among them freely and they had laughed and chatted while the girl's humanity had been stripped away. They were watching her now as the harsh reality of her face's imprisonment came home to her. She bobbed and weaved her head, her hands still bound behind her to her ankles and murmured forlorn pleas to her deity and her captors. Jokes were exchanged as the vodka continued to flow, and comments made over the comeliness of her breasts, the luxurious curve of her belly and the firmness of her ass. Even Drabik got into the spirit of the thing, speculating on her usefulness and expressing his interest in training her.

The messenger was carrying a leather satchel and he placed it in the middle of the encampment. The men who had shorn the former female reached into it and retrieved the pony's next accouterments.

One of the items was the standard ponygirl collar. Made of leather covered plastic, higher on one side than the other, it would lift her chin permanently so that, when she learned to pull a cart, her eyes would be just at the proper angle to the track in front of her as she leaned into her load. The men wrapped it around the pretty pony's slender neck and snapped it shut. It had little hooks on it so that the ponygirl hood could be pulled taut and affixed to it, further smoothing out the pony's former facial features. A strap hung behind the collar and once thick, leather bracelets had been affixed to the pony's wrists, her now vestigial arms were clipped on to it, one above the other. This enabled the pony to lay flat on her back for sleeping and fucking purposes without putting to much strain on her spine, while crossing them behind her would have had the opposite effect. The weight of her useless arms behind her on her collar forced the front up against her chin, keeping her head firmly in place.

Jerzi ordered Natasha to bring a leash and he had her lead the new ponygirl several times around the fire for the amusement of the men. The former young woman stumbled and staggered as she tried to get used to navigating through the tiny holes in her hood. The light played off her pale skin as her ample breasts bobbed and weaved. The former Zhanna cringed at the thought of her exposed, available body, so naked and helpless in front of these callous men. She had only ever been naked for her lover, Sergei, and one other before him. Now she would be naked for all the world. She gave out a desperate prayer in her mind that somehow she would find a way to escape. For now, she knew that she was these men's helpless prisoner and that they would do whatever they wanted with her.

She was still sputtering and crying as Grobgy took the leash from Natasha and pulled the ponygirl to his lap. He fondled her breasts and ran his hand over her tummy. He pressed open her thighs and took possession of her still hairy love lips and caressed and stroked them until the girl began to unwillingly lubricate. When his fingers were able to pass freely into her tight, wet crevasse, he plunged them deeply into her making her moan with unhappiness. He stroked them back and forth within her until she gave a little shudder of unwanted pleasure and then he took hold of the stiff bud atop her slit and gave it a mighty squeeze, making the pony groan with pain. The first lesson of a ponygirl: her masters could give her pleasure or pain. And they would decide which.

There was a little ceremony to perform and then Grobgy wanted to get back to his guests. The owners of the team that he would be racing tomorrow were at his mansion awaiting his return. He had left the heavyset, bearded man and his two sons in the care of several of his most delectable slave girls and he was sure that they did not miss him. But he had his duties as host and he didn't want to shirk them all night.

Grobgy ordered the men to finish denuding the girl of her human attributes. The men took hold of the dismally unhappy pony and forced her to her back on the ground. Natasha came out from the trailer with a bowl full of hot water, a bar of soap and a short, softly bristled shaving brush. The men already had a razor. One man held the pony down by her naked shoulders while two men took hold of her legs and stretched them widely. The black haired, almost scrawny, naked slave girl knelt by the new pony's hip and, leaning over her, began to soap the wiry bush between her distended thighs.

The girl's feet were towards Lightning and her cruel, vindictive owner and she watched with dismay as the slave girl began to shave away the young girl's pubic growth. It brought back painful memories to her of when her pudenda was first denuded of her adult hair, back in the slave center where she had first been brought on her arrival in this strange country. She still didn't know where she was, had never even heard of Kalikastan and only knew that the men spoke a guttural, difficult tongue that she presumed was Russian or Serbian or something like that. She watched as the curly, brown growth was whisked away by the razor. Natasha's hands were practiced at this task, having had the daily duty to shave the pussies of many a ponygirl during her numerous racing seasons as Jerzi's slave. She pulled the skin taut as she slid the razor expertly around the female's tender love lips, along the small area in the crux of her thighs, across her smooth, lower belly.

When Lightning's pussy had been shaved she had still considered herself a human being, referred to herself as 'Maddy', had no conception of the cruel purposes to which she would be put. Her heart went out now to the unfortunate, young girl. She recalled her pretty, innocent face, her carefree air, the whiff she had received of the girl's flowery perfume. Even though she had abused her, Lightning didn't wish this fate on anyone. She trembled as she rued her own condition, seeing it mirrored in the stripping of the unfortunate girl's humanity.

The pony's thighs quivered and shook as she struggled to avoid the denuding of her loins. She could feel the eyes of the men on her defenseless sex and knew that it was unlikely that they would resist its availability to their depredations for long. Her ankles were held in vice like grips by the men on either side of her and her back pressed down firmly into the earth beneath her. She could see the leering face of the man who had his hands pressed down on her shoulders as she looked up through her hood's tiny holes. As she felt the razor scrape away her pussy's growth, she closed her eyes and cried bitterly.

When Natasha was done, she knelt back and let the men have a good view of her work. The area around the former girl's exposed slit was colored a light red due to the irritation of her first shave there. Her love lips were slightly parted and the pink interior could just be seen. Grobgy ordered the slave girl to get the pony ready for him and the girl slid her hand across the pony's taut belly, the same area where her tattoo would be applied tomorrow, and then captured her love lips in her small, bony hand.

Natasha hated all of the ponygirls. If it weren't for them, she would still probably be living at the plush whorehouse that had first claimed her after her training. Jerzi had bought her there and she had been his dismally treated servant ever since. She had been pretty then, scarless and shapely. The demonic ponygirl driver made her what she was today and Natasha took it out on the ponygirls whenever she could, a fact that Lightning had learned to her dismay. She knew that the gangster was going to fuck the new ponygirl and she couldn't wait to hear the girl moan and cry as he plowed her with his thick shaft. She tickled the girl's love lips gently, separating them so that the men could see, teased the nubbin at its apex and then plunged her fingers deep inside her crevasse.

The young female who had been Zhanna writhed and moaned as she felt her sex tormented. The black haired slave girl leaned over and put her lips to her hardened clit and sucked on it until she gave out an involuntary moan from behind her gagged lips. The vulnerable ponygirl yanked and pulled on her ankles held firmly by the men in an attempt to deny the fiendish slave girl her access, but to no avail. When she felt the girl's tongue flicker rapidly on her sensitized clit, she gave a deep sigh of incipient passion and, realizing that she had thereby signaled to the men her readiness for them, gave out a heartfelt sob.

Grobgy rose when he heard the girl's sigh. He lowered his zipper and retrieved his thick, already hardened cock. It was his right as the new pony's owner to first use of her, a custom that he enjoyed heartily. He waved the slave girl away from the anxious, contorting pony and knelt between her thighs. He lowered his body over her and addressed his enflamed cock to her leaking, energized slit. Without fanfare, he pressed the head of his prick past her tender, engorged gates and slid inside.

The girl who had been Zhanna moaned with dismay as she felt the cock pierce her loins. The fat meat filled her, abrading her pussy's electrified walls and rubbing along her tingling clit. Her shoulders and ankles were released by the other men, confident that their boss could handle the slender, helpless ponygirl all by himself. She cried out as the man's coarse clothes scratched against her tender naked skin, burning the insides of her thighs and her tender lower belly.

Grobgy seized the pony's ample breasts in his hands and squeezed them as he plowed her soft, moist gully. He sucked hard at her nipples, one by one, driving the pony's lusts higher and higher. The creature writhed and squirmed beneath him in protest even as she moaned and sighed as his cock, lips and hands drove her lust.

Lightning watched with dismay and jealousy as she saw her owner ravish the new ponygirl. Her own loins started to burn as she imagined his thick tube within her tender cleft. Her nipples grew hard and she gave a low, lust inspired moan. She could only see the female's naked, pale legs and feet as her owner's vast, muscular body blocked the rest of the new ponygirl from view. Her bare heels dug into the ground on either side of the huge man's legs, dragging along and pumping back and forth in a feeble frog-like motion as she protested her use and sought desperately to push herself away from the tormenting cock. But the mass of the man who lay above her, his prick deeply sunk into her energized canal, was too big for her to move her body even one inch and her heels dug shallow, narrow channels in the hard packed dirt.

When Grobgy sensed the pony's crisis, he began to hammer his hips against hers. He could see the pupils of her eyes behind her hood's tiny holes darting back and forth in her dismay as her sexual energies prepared to crest. Grobgy had broken in a hundred ponygirls and he knew what he was doing. She would remember her first orgasm as a ponygirl and who had given it to her, something that she would share with every ponygirl who had ever been brought to his estate to be trained.

Zhanna peered up at the gleeful, callous face of her new owner. His face was rough and pock marked, he had a broad, long, bushy black moustache. His eyebrows were thick and wild and his eyes bore into hers like drills. She would remember this face as long as she lived, she was sure of that. And when her need began to crest and she moaned in forced passion, closing her eyes to absorb the intense pleasures of her cunt's contractions, she knew that the cruel face had been forever burned into her brain.

Lightning saw the girl's legs stop their resistance to her lusts. Her heels lifted into the air and her legs began to shake. She moaned loudly and then wrapped them around the back of the thighs of her owner, pulling him instinctively deeper into her convulsing crevasse.

When the bucking couple came to rest in the middle of the campsite, there was, for a few moments, an eerie silence. The men, usually so boisterous after the initiation of a new ponygirl, withheld their normal cheers. After all, a man had been killed tonight and a pretty, young girl, probably Russian, although no one knew her name, had been inalterably reduced to a servile creature right in front of them. Usually, the ponygirls arrived already shaven and hooded from the importer, having already suffered the initial stages of her dehumanization elsewhere. Unlike tonight, you didn't have to see their faces, had no concept of them as real, actual women. But this girl had been seen by all of them. In their minds they could still visualize her distraught features as she realized what was going to be done to her. She had worn clothing and the other accouterments of her humanity until a short while ago.

Lightning could hear the soft moaning of the former woman and the crackling of the raging fire as she knelt next to her driver. The sight of the poor girl being reduced to a life of cruel inhumanity was horrifying to her. It struck her to her core, reminding her of what she once was. How could these men do it, she thought miserably. How could anyone be so cruel? The horror of what had been done to her made her body shake. How could she possibly go on?

Grobgy rose from the body of his new ponygirl and zipped up his pants. He suffered no qualms as to what he had done. The girl deserved it. And what matter that this girl, as opposed to another, assumed the mantle of a ponygirl? Her body was lithe and attractive, her legs long and trim. Her breasts which lay in disconsolate pools on her chest were ripe and firm. She might be a little small for a ponygirl, but he was sure that Drabik would find some use for her. He watched her writhe for a moment at his feet, her legs drawn up and pressed together, her blue, hooded head moving side to side. She was a delectable sight.

The amoral gangster shook himself from his reverie and turned to his men. He had guests and he had to get back to them. "Anton," he said, addressing his prime henchman, "take her back to the pony barn and get her started. Give her a good whipping."

Drabik had risen to his feet as well. He nodded to his superior, disguising his resentment. He didn't need to be told what to do with a new ponygirl. A clear separation needed to be made for the ponygirls between their former lives and the lives they were now condemned to. Usually, they came to the estate already having been torn from a former life and tossed into a strange, uncertain sea. But this girl knew right where she was, what was going to happen to her. She may even have friends or family over at the public campsite awaiting her return. He would have to create the huge divide which would cleave, in the pony's' mind, all thoughts of her former humanity from her.

Drabik leaned over and, grabbing the ring in the new pony's collar, hauled her unceremoniously to her feet. Jerzi's black haired slave girl brought him a leash and he affixed it to the ring. He took a moment to examine more closely her smooth, enticing body. She swayed unsteadily on her bare feet. He was going to enjoy breaking her in. He then turned to look at Lightning, the pony who had cast a spell on him and saw her looking back at him. "Soon," he thought, "she will be mine." Turning his head, he yanked at the new pony's leash and began her trek to her new life.

Lightning continued to kneel forlornly in the shimmering light of the campfire as the men left. She released a soft sob as she watched the formerly happy and free, young girl disappear from the circle of light. Her driver, after rising to bid thanks and farewell to the other men, resumed his seat in his little chair, lit a pipe and resumed sipping his glass of vodka. All that was left of the horrifying scene that she had witnessed were the remnants of the girl's burning clothes in the campfire and a dark stain in the dirt where the young man's lifeblood had poured out of him.

After a while, her driver signaled to Natasha to prepare the pony for the night. The black haired girl took hold of Lightning's collar and pulled her to her feet. She was guided a distance from the encampment and allowed to crouch and pee. The slave girl was especially churlish in her handling of the taller, larger ponygirl as if assisting in the debasement of the pretty young girl had raised her own status.

Lightning slept, when weather permitted, on a thin cotton pallet underneath her driver's trailer. Natasha guided her to her spot and, once the pony had lain down on her back atop her bound arms, connected her collar to rings mounted in the ground on either side of her. Straps were wound around her thighs, binding them closely together. The slave girl removed her tall, black ponygirl boots and then connected her ankles together with a thin, leather thong. A chain connected them to a ring below her feet.

Since it had gotten cooler, Lightning had been given a thick woolen blanket to cover her during the night. Before stretching it out over her prone and imprisoned body,

Natasha took hold of Lightning's teats and gave them a cruel, painful tweak. The ponygirl looked up and saw her distorted, cruel face smiling evilly back at her. A wave of unhappiness coursed through her. Apparently satisfied at communicating her disdain for the ponygirl, Natasha released her nipples and cast the blanket over her, tucking it in under her sides. She then folded down the tabs over the small holes for her eyes, plunging the pony into complete darkness.

Lightning lay a long time, ruing her life, crying and sobbing. Her whole body was immobile, unable to do more than wiggle her toes or shift her shoulders or hips slightly from side to side. It was a sleeping posture she had long ago gotten used to, but tonight her bindings were especially loathsome to her. Above her, she heard her driver and his scrawny slave girl rutting like there was no tomorrow. The dwarf handled the girl roughly during their bouts of sex and tonight was no different. She could hear the girl wail and moan with pain and Lightning, for the first time, took some pleasure from the sounds of her torment. But later, as the dwarf got down to business, she felt a forlorn emptiness in her unused cleft as she heard the girl moan and call out her pleasure.

Once silence reigned again, Lightning's mind drifted back to what she had witnessed that night and to her own, previously repressed but now reemerging memories of her former life. Her heart felt like lead as she lay there bound into immobility as she recalled her boyfriend, the sometimes raucous tavern at which she once worked, her father, her friends. She had had her own apartment, had been attending community college. She didn't know what she really wanted to do with her life, but she had thought about nursing. All that was long gone and would never return. No one knew where she was, no one would ever rescue her. She didn't know what happened to ponygirls once their usefulness was through, but she knew that it was almost certainly an unhappy end. How could they ever return her to the status of a human being after what she had been through?

Tomorrow, she would race. The thought of the crowd's cheers, the thrill of running at a speed that made her heart pound and her body sing with pleasure turned to dust in her mouth. What did it matter? She had been seduced by the false thrill of being a champion. So what? In the end, she was just an animal to be treated with cruelty and disdain.

She had had a ponygirl lover once, a pony called Persephone. She had a long, thick, blond mane and large, pillowy breasts. They had run together as yearlings before Lightning had been reassigned to run the sulky. Those had been pleasant days and their driver often let them frolic together, giving each other pleasure with their lips and tongues. But Persephone had been sold, torn away from her several months ago by her owner's cruel, beautiful daughter. To her sorrow, Lightning had deduced that she was her trainer's mistress and the woman resented his attentions to the pony of which he had become more than enamored. The woman had treated Lightning cruelly and she knew that she was waiting out there for her. As soon as the racing season was done, she would again be subject to the woman's cruel depredations.

And her trainer. While her body craved his caresses, his attentions, she had seen him tonight as he looked over the tender body of the new ponygirl. Who was she kidding? He was a cruel, nasty man who would as soon whip her as fuck her. He had shown her some kindnesses, yes. But if her really cared for her, he would release her, free her. But that would never happen. He was as corrupted as he could be by his power over the forlorn creatures who had been reduced to human-like ponies.

What was the sense of living, the distraught young woman asked herself. Let them kill me, she thought. I want to die.

Lightning slept fitfully during the night. In the morning, she was awoken and released by Natasha and given her daily ablutions. But where she would normally be electrified by the knowledge that this was a racing day, her forlorn mood continued through her shower and the ritual denuding of her loins and scalp and the reinstallation of her black ponygirl boots. She docilely allowed the slave girl to roughly handle her, pushing and shoving her into the desired positions. When she was fed her bowl of oatmeal like cereal, she lapped it up obediently only to avoid the beating that she knew that she would receive from the girl if she did not.

Jerzi detected the sullenness of his charge. Ponygirls wore expressionless masks, and so she could not signal her unhappiness with a frown or a forlorn look. But there was something about the way she was acting, the way she held her shoulders, slouched as the slave girl ministered to her, that told him that something was wrong with her. He hadn't driven seven ponygirl champions because he didn't know how to handle a ponygirl. There was only one solution for her malaise.

Lightning was surprised when the slave girl bought out her whipping harness. It was made of leather and ran under her bound arms and across her back and chest. When affixed to the gibbet sunk into the dirt of the campground, it held her erect and vulnerable to her master's whip. As the girl tightened its cinches, Lightning began to cry. What had she done? Why was he doing this?

The slave girl dragged her to the gibbet and looped straps from the harness through a ring on each shoulder and then pulled the ponygirl to her full height so that she was standing on the tips of her heavy, ponygirl boots. Her driver was standing nearby, waiting, and holding in his small but strong hands the same lash he had used on the girl last night. Lightning moaned with fear as the slave girl set down in front of her the large, round platform that her driver used in order to reach her full height. He stood only a little over four feet tall and the ponygirl normally towered over him. Natasha was not much taller, maybe 5'1", while Lightning was a full 5'9".

Her driver mounted the platform and let the whip tear through the air so that Lightning could appreciate what he was about to deliver. Her feet were anchored to a ring in the ground so that she could not turn and avoid the angry lash. Her breasts seemed so exposed and vulnerable and she moaned as she anticipated the pain that they would soon suffer. "What have I done?" she asked herself miserably. "Why is he beating me?"

When the first blow from the lash ripped across her defenseless breasts, Lightning screeched with the pain from behind her gag. Her body stiffened and her hands behind her clasped together into fists. She tried to pull her feet free of their confinement but all that she achieved was a jerking of her body that made her burning breasts flutter and sway. The second blow fell across her taut belly. Her back arched back in anguish and she moaned loudly through her mouth's confinements, "Mmmmmmmmmmm! Mmmmm-mmmmmmmm!" The third kiss of the cruel instrument landed across her thighs. She rocked and swayed her hips in anguished response as the pain flowed through her.

Altogether, the cruel dwarf laid ten lashes across the pony's defenseless flesh. She screamed and yelled and danced in her bindings, tears flowing in streams down her face under her hood. When her large, firm breasts, her thighs and her belly were striped with bright red lacerations, he had the slave girl turn the pony around and he administered to her back, her rear and the back of her thighs. He even laid the long, hard lash across her hands, held prisoner behind her and useless except as a source of intense torment.

Long trails of red lined her body when he was done. Lightning sagged in her harness sobbing as her skin burned all over her body. "Ohhhhhhhh, god!" she cried to herself. "Why has this happened to me?"

The ponygirl felt her harness released from the gibbet and she swayed unsteadily as the slave girl released it from her body. She felt her training harness being applied in its stead and knew that she was about to be affixed to her cart for a training run. There was nothing less in the world that she wanted to do. But the burning of her lacerated flesh prevented her from making a single motion of resistance or protest. She hated being beaten more than anything. She was ashamed at how the mere presence of a whip would make her stomach go empty and her heart begin to beat wildly. It was how they ruled her. She would do anything to avoid the whip and just because she had already suffered an agonizing torment at her driver's hands didn't mean that it couldn't be renewed or that some other, more prolonged and painful suffering inflicted on her.

When she had been backed into the sulky cart, the poles connected to the belt at her hips, her shoulders and back affixed to the straps that led back to the cart, the slave girl forced her to her knees so that her bit could be installed. It was a thick, steel bar covered in leather and had a plate attached that cruelly and painfully depressed her tongue when the driver pulled on her reins. When it was belted tightly around her head, Lightning rose to her feet disconsolately. She felt the cart bounce slightly as her driver mounted it.

The unhappy ponygirl had a choice. She could stand in place, refusing to move, and suffer the wrath of her driver until she either succumbed and obeyed his instructions to move or was beaten into insensibility, or she could obey the flick of her reins and put her booted feet in motion, one after the other and head for the racing track as she had done many times before. When she felt the little tug on her bit, she hesitated for only a fraction of a second and then obediently went into motion.

All the way to the track the ponygirl cursed her cowardice. What the men had done to her was nothing compared to what she had done to herself. She had accepted her lowly, bestial status rather than suffer their cruelties. She had learned to revel in her use, obey their every command, eat and drink when ordered, shit and piss when permitted. It wasn't so much what the men had made her into, it was what she had allowed herself to become rather than suffer their cruelties. And here she was, servilely obeying the mere flick of the long, thin straps that led to her bit, striding along, towing her tormentor behind her.

A small crowd had already gathered in the grand stand when Lightning broke onto the track. Touts, aficionados, gawkers, all lined the rails to watch the ponygirls warm up for this afternoon's races. Lightning cursed herself as she passed them on her initial lope around the 1500 meter loop. Their eyes burned into her naked skin. She sensed them watching her attractive orbs as they danced on her chest, peering at her naked loins as she passed them, watching her without a single thought of her debased humanity intruding on their pleasure.

But, when her driver got her up to cruising speed, her thoughts of sorrow and unhappiness began to ebb. She could feel the comforting tread of her boots as they tore into the soft dirt of the track. Her breathing became rhythmic and heavy as she exerted herself. Her thighs began to warm with excited blood. Even the familiar sway and jump of her heavy breasts as they recorded each long, intense stride became comforting to her.

Normally, on race day, her driver did not let her open up to her full speed during morning warm-ups. There was no sense wearing the pony out. The run was just to make sure that she was without any physical impediments to her later performance and to get out of her system some of the usual and expected race day jitters. But this morning, Lightning felt her driver signal her through her reins to pick up her tempo. As she rounded the turn that led to the home stretch, her body went into automatic mode. The small crowd, seeing that her driver had accelerated her efforts, assembled next to the rail and a few called out their encouragement. By the time that she crossed in front of the reviewing stand, she was going full out.

Lightning exulted in the thrilling sensations of her exertions. All things passed from her mind but the need to place her strides out as far in front of her as they could go, to push as hard as she was able against the dirt beneath her boots, to raise and lower her strong, energized thighs as fast as she could. There were other drivers out on the track warming up their ponygirls and Lightning passed them as if they were standing still. When she passed the grandstand the second time, the assembled people were screaming and shouting. It was not something you saw every day. Warm ups were usually a rather laconic, uneventful prelude, but Lightning was turning it into a spectacle.

Lightning could hardly feel the bite of her driver's dressage whip on her back and rear as she pushed herself to her extreme. Dirt flew from her boots and rivulets of sweat poured from her body. Her teeth clenched madly on the leather covered bit in her mouth. Her legs ached and her lungs screamed with need as she went on and on and on. There was nothing else in the world but the idea of running, running, running. Nothing else mattered. Her brain was enraptured with the sensations that her body was sending her.

A large crowd had gathered at the rail on front of the grandstand when she made her final approach. Even the workers and slave girls had caught the enthusiasm, shouting and cheering her as she came on. When she crossed the finish line there was a huge roar and her mind exploded with joy.

As she took her cool down lap, Lightning could hear the crowd rhythmically calling out her name, "*Molnya! Molnya! Molnya!*" as they clapped in time. When she trotted back in front of the onlookers, her driver brought her into a canter and she pranced in front of them, her thighs raised high, each step poised and carefully executed. Her driver lifted his cap in salute to the fans and they cheered again. When they reached the end of the building, Lightning felt through her reins the signal to return to her trot from her driver and she began to lope back to the ponygirl encampment.

The ponygirl was covered with sweat and dirt when they reached the camp site. News of her performance had spread through the encampment and drivers and grooms saluted her and her driver as she passed down the narrow, dirt road. Jerzi ordered Natasha to release the still panting, joyous ponygirl from her traces and had her kneel down in front of him. He leaned over and released her bit, handing it off to the slave girl.

Lightning looked at her driver with wonderment. "How had he known?" she asked herself. That was just what she needed. All dismal thoughts were banished from her mind. Today was race day and, later, she would give the crowd more reasons to cheer. She watched as the small, caricature of a man withdrew his adult sized prick from his racing pants. He held it out to her and uttered words of encouragement, a sign that she was to take his flaccid, long, thick meat between her lips. She was surprised, but happy to be offered this treat. Obediently, Lightning inched herself forward on her knees and bent over. She spread her lips and subsumed the dwarf's member between them.

Lightning reveled in the feel of the man's hot meat in her mouth. She savored its salty taste as she suckled it gently and lovingly. He was truly the master of her. He had shown her the way out of her dismal unhappiness. She was a ponygirl, a champion. And although it was not by choice, she could celebrate her uniqueness, her unmatched abilities. She was like a comet streaking through the heavens, set on its course by some unknown force, doomed to burn out or collide with some other heavenly body and be extinguished. But while it burned brightly, it lit up the sky to the amazement of all who perceived it.

The dwarf's meat grew to hardness between the ponygirl's lips. She was crouched over low, her breasts touching her knees so that she could have access to his loins. She ran her tongue around the firm shaft and let her lips drift up and down, clamping them tightly against it. It was a rare pleasure, a signal of her driver's approval of her efforts. What happened last night was passed. The fate of the pretty, young girl who had been dehumanized before her eyes was none of her concern. She had only the pleasures that her masters could bring her. And to have her driver's manhood lodged between her lips, to be able to convey to him in the only way that she could her gratefulness for his understanding and mastery over her, was heaven itself. Her loins burned with need and her breasts ached as they filled with her excited blood. She heard the small man groan as he received her efforts and a thrill went through her. He placed his strong, gnarled hands on her blue clad, anonymous head and she moaned in return at the sensation of the contact, happy to let him guide her to his pleasure.

Lightning's cunt pulsed with her rising lust as the forceful hands of her master urged her head back and forth on his steel hard cock. She could hear the tell tale signs of his impounding crisis, the heaviness of his breathing, the rocking of his prick across her pursed lips. The soft textured but rock hard wand in her mouth made her delirious, like she was supping at the source of all power in the world. His fingers dug deeply into her head as his prick began to pulse and jerk in her mouth. When his salty, thick fluids began to jet from its end, she shuddered, her hands twisting behind her, her eyes jammed shut in joy. Her energized slit began to pulse and contract as she came too, moaning and crying, slurping delightedly on the dwarf's throbbing pole.

The small man's cock finally came to rest within her mouth and Lightning licked and suckled it until all of his discharge had dribbled from its tiny slit. She sighed with contentment as it left her lips. She looked up at her overlord's face and saw his understanding and the force of his masterly handling of her etched into it, his perception of her needs. She moaned with contentment as he slipped her gag back into her mouth, felt the large wad of leather fill her and her mouth sealed. She wasn't a woman anymore, she thought. What had she been thinking? She was a ponygirl.

That afternoon, Lightning beat her competitor by three lengths. Afterwards, her driver brought her back to the camp site, her neck bedecked with the winner's garland and fucked her fore and aft for two hours, bringing her repeated, intense, joyful orgasms.

CHAPTER THREE
TIME TO MAKE PLANS

Jake nibbled at the hardened bud of pleasure proffered tantalizingly above him as the slave girl's tongue and lips brought a wave of luxuriant pleasure to his cock. He was lying on his back, his knees up and his thighs spread wide, the lusting, black haired slave girl, Dana, lying atop, her knees on either side of his face, her smooth, hot thighs pressed up against his cheeks. He could feel her deliciously firm and plump breasts as they nestled against his taut belly, her fiercely hard nipples dragging across his sensitized skin as the girl shifted position to draw her lips down the length of his hardened pole or to lick at its bulbous tip. He was in heaven.

The early morning sun was bedazzling the room. He was in his bed in the cottage that had been allocated to him and his associates by Mr. Burnham, the estate owner. He had called a conference of his agents for 7 A.M. sharp, but he had awoken around 6 and had been fucking ever since.

There had been a shift in his relationship with the buxom, dark haired slave girl. She had been gifted to him by one of Burnham's contractors, undoubtedly in the hopes of obtaining his influence with the American billionaire. She, like Jake and Burnham, was an American, but unlike them, she was not a voluntary resident of the small, criminal run republic. In fact, although she did not know it, she had been brought to Kalikastan as a result of the slaving operation that Jake had taken over on behalf of Burnham as part of their plan to rescue Maddy. Jake had felt some discomfort at first with this thought as he used her, but by now he was fully over it.

The true discord in their relationship, if you could call it that, was the fact that immediately prior to her coming into his possession, another slave girl, Klara, a pleasantly endowed, blond, Dutch, former divinity student, had been stolen from him. Klara had been his first and only personal slave girl, the result of another gift when he had been posing as a ponygirl buyer and traveling from estate to estate in search of Burnham's niece. It had been an arduous task and he had been on the road for many weeks before he saw a telltale mole on the hip of a displayed, hooded and faceless ponygirl one night before a race. She had hair to match Maddy's. She was somewhat thinner in some places, her hips, for instance, and her thighs were much more developed. But he was sure it was her. He had whispered, barley audibly, her name as he passed her and the pony's confusion and consternation at the perhaps imagined sound of her name had confirmed his belief.

Klara had been a present from one of the estates from which he had made two ponygirl purchases in Burnham's name. He had been accompanied on the trip by Irkut, an old hand at ponygirls and an expert trainer. Irkut had been lured out of retirement by Burnham's money and was now head trainer on his estate. Klara was an innocent in a devilish world. At first, Jake was put off by the prospect of actually owning female flesh himself. The whole slaver bit was supposed to be a pretext to save Maddy. But the girl was enchanting in her simplicity and quickly became devoted to him. He had only beaten her once and, afterwards, sorrowfully, pledged to her to never do it again. He had not violated his vow.

And so he reveled in her company, treasured the possession of her warm, loving mouth with his prick, swam happily in her enthusiastic embraces as he plowed her soft, lustful furrow. But he knew two things. The first was that, no matter how much he wanted to believe it, her emotion for him was not love. Love is something given by a person free to give it or not. She was a slave girl and, not being free to say no to him, her affections could hardly be considered voluntarily given. The second was, no matter how much affection he had developed for her, when he left this place, as he knew that someday he would, there would be no way that he could bring her with him. He would have to abandon her to her fate, to be sold off to some cruel master, a whorehouse or worse. If she emerged free into the West, there would be no way to explain her disappearance to her family but the truth, and the powers that ruled this twisted land would never tolerate that. They might be able to conceal Maddy's reemergence into free society, but not hers.

Jake's dilemma was eliminated when Klara had been stolen while he was away on a trip with Burnham. It had been the same trip that he had received the gift of Dana on and his rage at his loss had overboiled. The former Ohio college student had suffered the brunt of his wrath as a symbol of his loss of Klara. He had treated as cruelly as any Kalikastani master, beating her and keeping her in a little cage in his room. But, over the last few weeks, he had begun to appreciate the humanity in her and had modified his cruel regimen of abuse.

Jake suspected that Anton Drabik was behind the theft of Klara. Under Kalikastani law, as a slave, Klara was not really a person, so you could not call it kidnapping. Jake had detected Drabik's suspicion of his and Burnham's bona fides at a banquet given by his boss, Grobgy, at the end of the spring racing season. Jake's theory was that he had stolen Klara so that he could get information from her on the American's real intentions in the country. He was certain that Drabik would have disposed of the pretty, innocent slave girl when he was through with her and he had sworn to himself that, if it was the last thing he did before he left the country, he would kill the man.

He had also sworn that he would never feel affection for a slave girl again, but he had felt his resolve slipping over the last few weeks. Her energetic and dedicated attention to his rampant pole right now was one of the benefits.

The dark haired girl's lips were bringing him a world of pleasure. He sighed deeply, in between his attentions to the fevered, leaking slit above him, as she slowly raised her lips up his swollen crank, washing it with her loving tongue and then slurping the fat head at the top. It was taking all of his effort to resist exploding into her hot mouth as her able lips and tongue drove his excitement higher and higher. He had made her come twice already. She had suspended, temporarily, her attentions to his prick, although maintaining it suitably lodged between her lips, while she moaned and her body shuddered with delight. Her thighs had clamped on his cheeks and she had pushed her engorged, hairless pussy lips down hard on his mouth as he tortured her little bud of pleasure with his tongue, flicking at it while he held her thighs firmly in place. When her ecstatic contractions ebbed, she regained control of her volitional functions and continued where she left off, energetically transferring the moist heat of her mouth and tongue to his cock.

However, it was getting harder and harder to prevent the eruption of his spunk. The slave girl's hand was cupping his soft, leathery sac and gently massaging his soft stones. She sucked hard on his prick while she drew her lips upwards slowly, as if she could pull his salty essence right out of him and then, opening her mouth wide, descended quickly upon him until his prick's meaty head pierced the edge of her throat and then repeated the exercise. His thighs began to tremble and he felt the telltale tingling in his balls and at the base of his prick. His hands gripped her soft, smooth, rear globes and he pushed his tongue deeply inside her crevasse, lashing at its soft, wet walls, reveling in the strong, pungent aroma of her discharge. The slave girl groaned with pleasure and the sound of her accelerating lust sent him over the top.

As his cock began to throb and jerk within the young girl's mouth, he seized her stiff clit with his lips and began a long, energized suck, rolling his tongue over and around the tiny, hard protuberance. Her thighs pressed firmly on the sides of his head and she began to thrust her hips at his face. She gave out a muffled cry, her voice stifled by his pulsing prick and he reciprocated, casting his pleasured groan deep into her canyon.

The sated couple lay entwined as their fires cooled. Jake took a last, long lick at the slave girl's flush quim, sending a reminiscent tremor through her body and then eased her legs aside and rose from the bed. He looked at the clock and saw that he had ten minutes before his meeting. Just enough time for a quick shower and to throw on some clothes.

The slave girl Dana was still lying face down on the bed and he, without giving it much thought, clipped her wrists between her back and her ankle bracelets together. He may have softened in his attitude to the enticing, voluptuous slave, but that didn't mean he wanted her running around all over the place. She was still a slave girl and he was her master, her owner, in fact. Hard as that was, in Kalikastan it was the cruel reality. She would never be more than a slave girl and there was no sense creating any false impressions in her. He might be a 'fellow American' and all that, but that only meant that they had seen some of the same TV shows.

Jake washed his body quickly and efficiently and then threw on a fresh pair of boxers, some jeans and a t-shirt. After he had slipped on his socks and a pair of heavy, light brown work boots, he unfastened Dana's ankles and, giving her ass an affectionate, loud slap, ordered her from the bed.

Dana had jet black hair that went down to her shoulders, straight and thin. Her face was oval shaped and she had Betty Boop lips. Her eyes were light blue and her skin pale. Her breasts were round, firm and sizable on her medium frame. She had lost some weight while a prisoner in his second story bedroom in the small cottage and he had determined that she should fatten up a bit and get some exercise. The slave master over at Burnham's sprawling mansion held exercise classes for the slave girls two times a day, at 10 and at 3. He would send her over later. But for now, she had to go back into her cage.

Jake picked up the girl's gag from the bed where he had tossed it earlier and proffered it to her lips. She hesitated briefly, but obediently accepted it. He tightened it behind her head.

"One of the girls will be up with your breakfast later," he told her. "At ten you're going over to the mansion for a workout. Be a good girl and don't let me hear any complaints about you. Do whatever you're told. Understand?"

The silenced girl gave a doleful nod. Jake took hold of her heavy orbs and caressed them. "This afternoon, you can spend some time downstairs with the other girls." Dana's breasts carried light red markings where he had whipped her this morning before supping at her loins. He no longer beat her from anger, but once you have watched a beautiful girl sobbing and moaning at the end of your whip, it's hard to give it up. He had merely toasted them a little bit as an encouragement to her efforts and his prick.

In fact, Dana had become quite used to being tormented by the mid sized, brown haired man. Once she had gotten over the worst of it, she had discovered that a slight tanning encouraged her passions to come to a boil. It was always helpful to have something to engage your lusts, especially since a lack of sexual ardor was a punishable offense in itself. She had decided that, after all, this guy wasn't as bad as some of the others that she had heard about and, now that he was giving her more and more freedom, being his property was a lot better than things could be. At least, for the most part, she had only one man to serve rather than the huge variety she had entertained when the property of the caterer who had bought her and trained her. And he was an American so that he spoke English and she could understand his commands. He had had her fuck his men last week, and that had not been too bad. They were kindly and appreciative of her efforts. Her hardships as a slave girl were getting towards a tolerable level. Some day, she had pledged to herself, she would escape. But until an opportunity arose, and you had to be careful, a failed escape was much worse than none at all, life with the man they called Jake was not that bad.

Jake opened the door to Dana's little steel home and encouraged her in. The bottom was padded and there was just room enough for her to turn around in it as she knelt awaiting her next call to service or to lay down scrunched up into a little ball if she wanted to sleep. She watched as her master took a 3' long, thin, riding crop down from the wall. He placed it in the cage with her.

"This is for later today. I'm going to stripe your ass and then fuck you there until you come," he told her, smiling.

Her belly quailed at the thought of her impending abuse, but, at the same time, her pussy gave a little twinge at the thought of the man's fat cock up her ass. Now she had something to look forward to.

Everyone was assembled in the little kitchen of the cottage when Jake arrived at 6:55. All of the slave girls, who tended to accumulate in the small house, service here being a pleasure compared to back at the big house, had been shooed away. Martinez, and Curley were sitting at the table, while Tucker, a mountainous sized man with short, crew cut hair, was pouring himself a cup of coffee. Jake looked out the window and saw a pair of pale, white, blond tailed ponies hitched to a cart. They didn't belong to Tucker, although they might as well have. He had taken over the care of the two older, heavyset ponies after Burnham had acquired them second hand last spring. They were former racers, pulling a large landau as part of a nine pony team. They had large, muscular thighs and thick shoulders. The seller told them that they had been ponies for about seven years. Pulling the landau required considerable strength and over time the calves and thigh muscles just couldn't take the strain. But the pair, who had been christened Dora and Flora when they were dehumanized, were still good for pulling small loads around the estate and for carefree rides out in the country. Burnham took them out for a spin most mornings that he was home. But it was Tucker, who had grown quite enamored of them, who cared for them, massaging and grooming them, taking them out for frequent exercise and keeping them well fucked.

Leon was there too. He and Curley, who got his name due to his resemblance to his comic namesake, were pals. If you wanted one, you had to take the other. They weren't particularly skilled at anything, but they were loyal and they obeyed orders.

Finally, there was Irving. It would have been difficult to look for a person who seemed more out of place with the tough, experienced 'fixers' of Jake's team. He stood about 5'5" in his shoes and he wore thick, round rimmed, steel frame glasses. He had a bony face and the remnant scars of adolescent acne on his face. But Irving was as smart as a whip. He was Jake's tech guy, solved all of the scientific problems and also, sometimes, provided Jake's team with the 'can do' tools necessary for their various tasks.

Jake was worried about his team though. They had been sitting around high on the hog for seven months. Naturally, they had quickly fallen into step with the slave culture of the lawless country. Martinez, a lanky Latino, good with a knife and absolutely fearless, was the most serious offender, as the girls seemed naturally attracted to his rough, good looks, his Latin insouciance and his thick cock. While Leon and Curly had had a few favorites over the months, Martinez seemed to have a new favorite every week.

The boys had all been paid handsomely by Burnham while 'in country'. Burnham, at one point, wanted to send them home, but Jake had argued successfully against that. Burnham had been relying more and more heavily on his Russian security chief, Ilya Boradin. Jake convinced Burnham that it would be a good thing to have some Americans around to balance the crafty Russian out. Since then, the two security teams had played a kind of cat and mouse game, carefully monitoring each other's movements and reporting back to their respective chiefs.

But where were his team's loyalties now, he wondered. How would they take the news that soon they would be going back to the world and leaving this satyr's paradise behind? Would Curly and Leon insist on rescuing their current beaus? Would Martinez ever want to leave? And Tucker, what would he do? He was enamored with the two, large ponygirls in his care. He had knocked a groom about viciously for whipping them one day. How would he react to the fact that they would be back in the hands of caretakers whose affection for them no way matched his nor his reticence at issuing them abuse.

And then there was Irving, always the odd man out. When they had raided the farm where Maddy had been held, they had found a slightly roly poly girl there locked in a cage underground. Her name was Maureen and Irving wanted to release her to her undoubtedly distraught family. Jake had nixed it. Their only chance of saving Maddy was if the guys who had her didn't know they were on their trail. Maureen's homecoming after weeks of captivity would have set off all kinds of alarm bells. The FBI would get involved and would upset the applecart. So, after receiving permission from Burnham, Jake agreed to let Maureen be held at some private sanitarium as an anonymous patient until the rescue of Maddy was complete. When Maddy was found and brought home, Maureen could be released.

That seemed to be an adequate solution to the matter for Irving, but Burnham fucked it up. His concern was Maddy and only Maddy. He didn't give a shit about Maureen or any other of the girls who had been kidnapped. Rather than continue her as a security risk, he had, without telling Jake, hired some guys to drop her in a hole.

For the next few months, Irving, who had been left behind in the States to run his lab, had bugged the shit out of Jake. "Where's Maureen?" he would ask insistently. No matter how often Jake told him that her location was a security matter, three days later, Irving would be on the phone again. "Where's Maureen? Where's Maureen? Where's Maureen?" Jake had gotten sick of it and had asked Burnham for the information. Burnham's reticence to release the information told Jake one thing. Maureen was dead. Burnham had had her killed a rather than risk a leak on the operation to save Maddy.

But Jake had been wrong about that. They needed Irving's services as part of the new plan they had hatched to bring Maddy home. Maddy's owner, Grobgy refused to sell her, understandably since he was in no need of money and she was, after all, a champion. And Burnham had killed the idea of snatching her. So, they had decided to recruit their own ponygirl to challenge Maddy to a match race. If their ponygirl won, they would get Maddy, or Lightning, as she was now called. If they lost, Grobgy would get access to millions of dollars of graft on Burnham's pipeline. They needed Irving to even up the odds somewhat to make technological changes to the standard sulky racing cart to give their pony an edge. Irving's price was Maureen. Not only had the techie refused to help unless Maureen was produced, he threatened to go to the FBI and the newspapers and blow the whole thing unless the big boned, heavy set girl was brought here to him in Kalikastan where he could be sure that she was indeed alive and well.

It was a good thing that Burnham had hired some real crooks. Rather than killing Maureen as they had been hired to do, they her sold her off to a whorehouse in Mexico, thereby getting paid on both ends. For a considerable consideration, they told Burnham where Maureen was and the billionaire was able to have her brought to Kalikastan to satisfy Irving.

But there was the rub. Maureen had suffered horribly while a whore in Mexico. The madam there, despaired of making the somewhat homely, fat girl a good whore had, in a moment of inspiration, converted her into a pig. She had been shaved and made to walk around on all fours. They had glued a pig's nose and ears to her hairless head and even implanted a small, curly tail in her rear. She was fed thousands of fatty calories every day to make her blow up in size, way beyond her normally dumpy dimensions. Wearing hoof like shoes on her hands and knees, her ankles buckled to her thighs, she had, indeed, looked just like a pig and was the delight of the special parties that the madam conducted. With an injection into her vocal chords, the unfortunate girl even sounded like a pig as she squealed when they made her come or whipped her.

So, when Maureen came to Kalikastan she weighed upwards of 250 pounds, too big to wear the huge house dress that Jake had picked up for her. Her psyche had been so damaged that she actually rued being returned to womanly status. Everyone wanted to fuck La Taconera Cochina, the whore pig. No one wanted to fuck a hugely obese, homely woman. She had resisted all of Irving's attempts to comfort her. When she saw some of the ponygirls being hitched up to the large cabriolet carriage one day, she had found her solution. The ponies were big and strong and trim and appealing. Maureen decided then and there that she wanted to become a ponygirl and she wouldn't take no for an answer.

With some reluctance and, to the amusement of Burnham and most of the trainers and grooms, Maureen had gotten her wish. She was stripped and hooded, tattooed and shaved. She now resided in the ponygirl barn with the rest of the ponies that were not engaged in any of the racing teams.

So what would Irving do now? Would he return to the States without Maureen? Would he blow the whole gig? After all, if Burnham had kept his word, Maureen wouldn't have been made into a pig nor would she then have wanted to become a ponygirl. Irving was quiet and taciturn and, for all Jake knew, might be planning to fuck Burnham right up the ass. In the meantime, Burnham insisted that he remain in Kalikastan for the duration of the fall pony season. But what would he do when Jake told them of their plans to go?

Jake called the conference to attention. His first question was for Irving.

"Have you swept the cottage?"

"As you asked, Jake. I do my job. Okay?"

"Okay, Irving, okay,' Jake replied somewhat defensively. "I need to know for sure. That's all."

He looked at his assembled crew.

"The racing season is over in two days. The Fall Tournament begins in about ten and lasts three days. If Grobgy takes the bait and agrees to run Maddy in a match race, it'll probably take place the day after that. So we've got two weeks to firm up plans to get her out of here."

Jake looked around to gauge the effect of his comment on his men. Their eyes shifted around the room and they were shuffling their feet.

"Okay," he said. "What's the matter?"

There was a moment's silence and then Leon spoke up. "I don't want to leave Chelsea behind." Chelsea was the name of his current paramour, a buxom, blond girl from Brixton. Leon said the same for his girl, Marissa, a tall, thin Italian beauty. The room was dead silence.

After a few moments, Jake spoke. "There's only two women who are leaving here with us when we go. One of them is Maddy. That's why we came in the first place. The other is Jackie." Jackie was the tall, young brown skinned, African American whore Jake had recruited to be their ringer. Her kidnapping had been faked and she had been shipped to Kalikastan to be made into a pony girl. She had been renamed Chocolate and was currently representing the Burnham estate as a sulky runner. And doing quite well at that. He had promised Jackie a million dollars to become a pony girl for the five months that the scheme would take. And then to return her to the States. Jake never broke promises.

Leon and Curley had their heads downcast. Jake continued. "We came here to do a job. You've been paid good money. What happens here is none of our business. We can't rescue anyone else without fucking up the whole thing. And you guys gave me your word. I take that very seriously." Nobody had to tell the boys what Jake meant when he said that he took something very seriously. Men who ignored what Jake took seriously risked serious health problems.

Tucker, who talked as if every word cost him money, spoke out in a low, determined voice. "I'm not going," he said. From his tone, Jake knew that his decision was final.

"What about you, Irving?" Jake asked his technician. "Are you coming or staying?"

Irving looked up at Jake with uncharacteristically steely eyes. He had not forgiven Jake for fucking up where Maureen was concerned, even though it was Burnham who had actually done the dirt on her. But, in Irving's opinion, Jake should have done something to rescue Maureen once he knew that Burnham had lied.

"I don't know, Jake," Irving returned. "Maureen wanted to be a ponygirl. I wonder if she still does. There was no way that she could have known what it was really like. My guess is that she's changed her mind long ago but, like all the other ponygirls, has no choice in the matter now."

"Listen, Irving," Jake retorted. "She was told before she became a ponygirl that it was permanent, that there would be no reprieves. That was her decision. She'd been here long enough to see how they were treated. I'm not taking her with us and that's final."

"Oh, so that's final, eh, Jake," Irving retorted. His ire was up, something unusual for the normally sedate, reserved scientist. "I guess that it's as final as your word that she would be okay while we did the search for Maddy. And like your word that the slaving operation back in Jersey would only last a couple months. You knew that I was against that, but, nooooo," he said with dramatic emphasis, "you said we had to do it. That the girls who were being kidnapped would have been taken anyway. How many girls have come over from the States through your operation, Jake? How much of their tears and screams of pain are on your hands? How many innocent young women are going to bed tonight, thinking that they will have the opportunity to be free and independent persons, to go to school, have lovers, children, make something of themselves, but will find themselves bound and gagged in a cage tomorrow on their way to a life of cruelty and degradation?"

Enough was enough. While Irving talked a big game and had, initially, refused to have anything to do with the slave girls, that resolve had lasted all of one day. Now, he, like the others, enjoyed the services of the highly trained sexual thralls on a more than daily basis.

"Listen Mr. High and Mighty," Jake answered him, "you haven't kept your dick in your pants. Or do the girls who come up to your room play tic tac toe with you all night? You knew what you were getting into when you agreed to provide me with your services. I gave you that choice back in Georgia. In or out. And you wanted in. That was your word to me and I'm going to hold you to it. And so will Burnham. And if you think that you can blow the lid on things here and back in Jersey, you've got a lot of thinking to do. Who do you think that Burnham has been talking to all this time on that big conference screen of his? His therapist? No, he's knee deep in shit here but he has the full blessing of the powers that be. They're running prisons here, channeling back door payments to foreign governments, doing what they can't do under the light of day or the scrutiny of Congressional committees."

Jake halted to catch his breath. The naiveté of his scientist astounded him. "And if you blow the whistle, do you think that it will be just you they'll go after? They won't stop there. They'll hold you prisoner while every day bringing you news reports of your whole family being wiped out, one by one, sisters, brothers, cousins, nieces and nephews. Would you like to see one of your pretty little nieces bent over a whipping stand at a whorehouse down in Dlitski? Or running the 1500 meter yearling race? Wake up, Irving. School is out."

There was a deadly silence in the room. Irving absorbed the truth of Jake's statements. He had threatened Burnham with exposure but he knew now that it was just a bluff. And he had been given a choice by Jake. He knew that Jake was a 'whatever it took' kind of guy. And working with him just a nudge over on the wrong side of the law had given him a thrill, something to spice up the normally staid and dull aspects of his profession. But he had to draw the line somewhere. And that somewhere was with Maureen.

"I'm sorry, Jake," he said lowly. "I won't help on the escape unless Maureen gets the chance to come along. If she says no, then fine. But I owe her that much and you owe that much to me. You promised that she would be okay."

The slightly built but strong and wiry fixer stood silent for a moment. He had promised, and his word was his bond. And they needed Irving desperately if they were going to pull it off, if any of them were going to get out alive. "Okay, Irving," he said finally. "We'll give Maureen the choice." He turned to look at Leon and Curley. "But that's all. No one else."

Jake looked over at the up to now silent Martinez. "And what about you?"

"I'm with you Jake, all the way. Until the job's done. Once Maddy and the others are on their way out of here, I'll do whatever you say. But at that point, it's up to me to go or stay. I'll let you know then."

That was good enough for Jake. He looked back at Tucker. "And you, Tuck," he said. "Can we count on you, even though you're staying? I can't guarantee what they'll do to you after we leave."

The taciturn Tucker merely nodded his head.

"Okay, then," Jake said. "Here's the plan."

CHAPTER FOUR
ONE FOR THE ROAD

The spanking new slave training center on Burnham's estate had been formally opened a month ago. They had moved the operations from the cellars of the Burnham mansion about ten days prior, so that the kinks could be worked out and all systems tested. Everything had worked fine and the 'charter class' so to speak, a mixed bag of some American girls, two Italians, a young French woman and three coffee colored Brazilians had been received in a little ribbon cutting ceremony attended by Burnham and a representative of the Ruling Commission.

The building itself was set about a quarter mile from the mansion in the direction opposite from the public pony racing course and associated facilities. Nestled in a clump of tall evergreens and designed to mimic a modern American corporate office, it was one story above ground, consisting of administrative and reception functions, a show room and a communications center, and three floors below. There would be no escapes from the underground training area as there was only two ways up, a highly secured elevator and a set of emergency stairs access to which was governed by alarmed doors. Just to get to the elevator or the emergency staircase, you had to go through two, large, steel doors with guards permanently stationed at each. No freshly captured, disorientated young woman, assuming she could free herself from her cell or from the particular training pod that she was held in for her intermittent sessions with the staff, could hope to pass through them without an escort and clear, written authorization from administration.

Each underground floor specialized in a separate phase of the process of turning a frightened, young kidnapped female into a willing, enthusiastic, sex slave. The bottom floor was used for Stage One. This is where the girls, once they had been examined and their physical qualities recorded in reception, would be dealt with first. They were always brought down alone, regardless of how many subjects they had been brought in with. The slow descent to the bottom floor was important in demonstrating to them the hopelessness of their new condition. Naked, gagged and collared, their wrists encircled in their first set of slave bracelets and fastened behind them, their ankles connected by a 18" long chain and with two large, muscular, male guards on either side, the impossibility of avoiding their fate was driven home starkly.

Once they had reached their destination, they were hustled off immediately to the marking department where they would receive their distinctive tattoos and have their pubis shaved and ringed. Rather than depending on a trainer to come up with a new name for the imbonded sluts, the marking department worked off of a list, and the new name that a slave girl received was based on what name was next up, giving some consideration to the young woman's nationality and her perceived nature. This did away with the numerous Veronicas, Katyas, Tulips and other names favored and repeated too often by the trainers.

The new girls were housed in a tiered bank of small cells set into the wall. They were built three rows high and ten across, making room for 30 slaves in the initial stages of training at one time. The cells were constructed of specially hewn, light reddish, granite brick. They were each about four feet high, four feet wide and four feet deep. They were fronted by thick steel bars, each about four inches apart. At the press of a button on the outside or at the control desk next to the bank of cells, the bars extended to close the gap between them so that the cell could be plunged into darkness.

The bottom of each cell was covered with a rubberized mat that served also as a sleeping surface for the inmate. The floor sloped downwards slightly to the right hand corner of the cell where there was a bidet that could be used as a toilet. When it was time for a slave girl to be washed, or merely to add to her torment and dismay, soapy water could be jetted out of nozzles built into the walls followed by a clear rinse. The residue would roll down the slight incline to the bidet. A television screen was built into the back wall on which the inmate could watch videos of her own use and torments, or of other females who had come before them. Locked alone in their shuttered, pitch dark cells for long periods of time, their attentions would be drawn naturally to the activities on the screen, no matter how horrifying or repulsive to their natures.

Every cell had clear view of the whipping post mounted in the middle of the large area in front of them. Of course, with so many new slave girls to deal with, whippings were common. All of the girls who were in their cells at the time were expected to come to attention and press up against the bars while a punishment was in progress. Each girl was given a sound thrashing there on the day of her arrival after first being made to see the other imbonded women, gagged, bound and naked, peering out at them from the little cells. The new subject would be left ungagged so that all of the others could hear her desperate screams, her cries and sobs and her frantic, futile pleas for desistance. The wall across from the cells was lined with a huge mirror, extending from ceiling to floor. This way, when the habitués of the tiny cells looked out, they could see themselves and the cells belonging to all of the other unfortunate guests of the training facility as well.

One of the rules of Stage Three was that there was no talking. By anybody. The new slave girls existed in a world of silence, except for the echoes of theirs or another's yells and screams as they were whipped or beaten. All of the commands from the guards were given non-verbally, by a clap of the hands, the snapping of fingers or by the pointing of a whip or riding crop. It was a system that resulted in frequent corrective instruction as the girls tried to decipher what they trainers or guards wanted them to do. But it did make them particularly attentive to each nuance of the men who governed them.

The whole system, including the routines that took place in the training rooms, was designed by a team of behavioral psychologists retained by Burnham. One, an older scientist with a full professorship at Harvard, had several best selling, behavioral modification self help guides to his credit, and the woman, a professor at the University of California, Berkeley, was a talk show host on the Fox Network. They had been intrigued by the challenge, and now everything that happened to the poor, unfortunate women who had been deprived of their lives and their liberties was dictated by the manuals written by the two psychologists. They had both been on hand for the grand opening and had agreed to weekly visits to the facility so that the programs they had designed could be revised and updated based on actual experience and so that adjustments could be made in individual cases, if need be. As guests of the estate, of course, they had free pick of their nightly companions.

The watchwords of the bottom floor of the training center were pain and abuse. Nothing was really expected from the pretty, unfortunate inmates at this stage other than an absence of resistance to the men who invaded their bodies, often in ways that had not experienced before, and the suffering of pain. The pain was either blatantly physical, through the frequent and harsh torment of their flesh with the varied whips and riding crops available to the trainers, or merely psychological, the long times isolated in the darkness of their sealed off cells, watching the torment of themselves or their sister captives on the TV screen, or being continually bound and confined. And then, of course there were the markings and rings on their flesh. The permanency of their new condition had to be given time to sink in.

Once sufficiently stripped of their prior psyches, the girls would be moved up to the second floor where, pursuant to the protocols of Stage Two, training would continue, but be more particularized as to their participation in the carnal acts which would be their primary purpose from here on in. And, when they had been shown to be consistently enthusiastic and willing, and when their skills met acceptable standards, they would move to the third floor, Stage Three, where they would learn the etiquettes of service, acting out a simulacrum of their probable future existence once they had fully graduated and were either sold to an individual owner or shipped off to some brothel. The trainers lived on the third floor and there were rooms where guests of the estate or its leaders could enjoy the tongue and lips of a slave girl on the brink of graduation or make use of the gap between her thighs or the small, now rendered easily penetrated, aperture in her rear.

Burnham was proud of the state of the art facility. He already had plans to build a similar one for a training house in the capital. He was here today to make sure that everything was set for tomorrow when there would be a pony race on the estate. Several potential buyers had indicated that they would be happy to drop by and look at his stock and Burnham wanted to make sure that everything would be tip top. Nine females had been certified as ready for sale, the first crop who had passed their entire training in it.

Burnham drove himself over to the training center using Dora and Flora, admiring the movements of their powerful, naked haunches as they trotted along. He hitched them to a post near the entrance and walked inside. The male receptionist greeted him and called the superintendent of the facility out to meet him. The reception area was large and well decorated, with several comfortable chairs, a sofa and a magazine rack that contained, among other things, a catalogue with pictures and descriptions of the current trainees and their estimated ready dates. The cover had a picture of the emblem of Burnham's estate, the head of a black, snarling, vicious mastiff, with blood red teeth and eyes. Underneath was the facility's motto, "We will sell no slave before her time."

Burnham shook the hand of the tall, lanky superintendent when he emerged from his office. He was Kalikastani, with a dark complexion and a long, thin, bony face. His short, black hair was streaked with grey as was his large, bushy moustache. He was a cousin of Khalid, who had recommended him. He was dressed in a western style shirt and tie and suit pants over a pair of shiny, black shoes. Just the professional style that Burnham preferred.

"Good morning, Barouf," Burnham said as he shook the long, skeletal hand of the superintendent.

"And to you, Mr. Burnham," the man returned. "All is in readiness. Can I get you a coffee or other refreshment?"

"No thanks," Burnham replied. "Let's just get down to business.

Standing next to Barouf was Allen Pinter, an American recruited by Burnham to learn the trade. He acted as Barouf's assistant.

"Good morning, Mr. Burnham," he said, smiling and extending his hand. Burnham grabbed it without returning the greeting. He wasn't sure about Pinter. Time would tell. His experience was that Americans were too queasy to be good slave trainers, not that they balked at the use of the final product. You had to be a hard man to impose the tribulations necessary for effective slave education and he didn't think that the slightly built, mousy man had what it took. But he served a double function of keeping an eye on things. The men who staffed the facility were mostly Russians, with some native Kalikastanis to assist them. Burnham didn't fully trust any of the foreigners in his employ.

They walked the finely appointed hallway into the facility towards the showroom. The rug was a plush maroon and there were prints on the walls, erotic, but tasteful. They entered a large room with a series of stuffed easy chairs set around it. There were little polished, mahogany tables and a credenza along one wall decorated with a large vase full of flowers. A nude slave girl knelt next to the credenza her thighs spread and her hands folded behind her back. She wore blond tresses that descended to her shoulders and had a pretty face.

"I don't like that," Burnham stated flatly as they entered the room.

"What?" Barouf asked, his tone offended.

"The slave girl. She shouldn't be here. She'll just distract the buyers. Get her out."

Barouf snapped his fingers and the girl leapt to her feet. Her large breasts swayed as she fled. She had heard the tone of the big, English speaking man and wanted nothing to do with him.

"But who will serve the guests refreshments?" asked Baruof.

"You do it," Burnham replied. "It'll help you establish some intimacy with the buyers. And only tea or coffee. I don't want any drunks handling the merchandise or hanging out any longer than they need to to make a purchase."

"As you wish, Mr. Burnham," Barouf replied.

The tall, big boned American sat in one of the easy chairs and looked around the room. He was wearing a pair of tan slacks and a yellow, short sleeved sports shirt with his emblem on its pocket. "The room looks okay," he said. It was softly lit except for a small spotlight that brightened the center of the room. The walls were a comforting baby blue and the ceiling was white. Several prints of delectable, young women hung on the walls, showing them in various forms of restraint. Across from him was a large mural of a woman in the throes of passion. Her head was tossed back and her knees were raised, her thighs spread. Her hands were holding her large, bulbous breasts and her lips were parted as if in ecstasy. Her body filled the entire wall. Her huge, three foot high pussy appeared dilated and wet between her open thighs. Burnham gave it a cursory glance. "Give me the sales book," he demanded curtly.

Barouf, who had taken a seat next to Burnham, presented his employer with an 8½" x 14" binder adorned with the estate logo and the motto of the training facility. He flipped it open to see an arrangement of the photos of the nine young women who had been found to meet the facility's high standards. They were all naked and kneeling in a standard submissive pose. The camera work was excellent and you could see their faces clearly and their pleasant breasts and taut bellies. Their hairless slits were slightly parted as a gesture of invitation. You could tell that the women were aroused by the flushed faces and the glistening between their thighs. Their lips were all open as if in passion and their eyes met the viewer with a frank expression of their availability.

"Very good," Burnham announced. "I like it."

"It's Mr. Pinter's work, Mr. Burnham," Barouf answered. "He put the photos together. Keep looking, you'll enjoy it."

The American billionaire paged through the rest of the photographs. Each, desirable, young woman was shown in a variety of poses. There was an identification of their nationality, their slave name and their age as well as their bodily measurements. Several of the pictures showed the women engaged in sexual acts, a man's thick cock in their mouths or bent over and being fucked from the rear. "I don't want these in here," Burnham stated. "It just reminds the buyer how many times the sluts have been fucked. I want them to think, or imagine anyway, that there all clean and pristine. They'll know it's not true, but why remind them that they're essentially used."

"I'll put some different shots in, Mr. Burnham," Pinter said eagerly. He wanted to impress the demanding billionaire. He had remained standing. "I have some others. How about ones with them all bound up or being whipped."

"Bound up I like," Burnham replied. "But whipped no. Just use some shots with them holding whips in their teeth or something like that."

"No problem," Pinter answered. "I can do some more shots this afternoon."

Burnham slammed the binder closed. "Okay, show me the merchandise. I don't need to see them all. Let me see, let's say…," he paused while he reopened the binder to the first page, "Number 3 and Number 7."

Barouf lifted a phone from the table next to him. "Send in Number 3 and then Number 7," he intoned softly.

A few moments later, a soft, melodious music filled the room. It had a languorous beat. It was, in fact, a traditional Kalikastani love balled performed by one of the native orchestras down in Dlitski. A moment after the music started, a panel opened in the wall opposite where Burnham sat, just between the outstretched thighs of the sultry and excited woman in the mural. A pretty, young, blond haired girl crawled out of it. It looked just like the girl was emerging from the painted woman's pussy.

Burnham laughed heartily. "I like it! I like it!" he said. It's just the right touch!"

Barouf smiled happily while the girl, now fully emerged, rose to her feet and began a slow, sultry dance before the men. She had long, full, wavy, blond hair that reached to her hips. Her breasts were pale and full, with hardened points on them. Above them, tattooed on her chest in two inch high, florid letters, was her name, Marina. Her pussy was bare, and when she moved and spread her legs, you could see the small golden medallions dangling from her love lips. For now, they were blank. Later, they would contain the insignia of her buyer.

Burnham watched, transfixed, as the woman danced before him. She rubbed her breasts and licked her full, plump lips. She ran her hands down her sides and over her thighs and then rubbed them between her legs, pinching her denuded, fat labial lips together with the sides of her hands and then releasing them. Her moisture of arousal sparkled in the overhead spot light. She turned and bent in half with her legs spread, curling her arm underneath her until it appeared between her thighs. She rubbed her pussy, making a little circle over her rigid bud of pleasure and then plunging two of her fingers inside her. She thrust her long, thin fingers back and forth, further exciting her plush canal. At some signal from the music, she turned and smiled broadly at Burnham and then took up a kneeling position on the side of the room about five feet away from him.

The music continued, shifting to a slightly more excited beat. Number 7 emerged from between the painted woman's legs. She had short, black hair, done up in ringlets around her head. Her face was sharp and narrow and possessed a certain impishness. Her eyes flashed blue. Her skin was paler than the blonde's, almost pasty, but it was accentuated by a thin line of black hair around her love canal. Her lips were painted a bright red as were her long fingernails, the lips of her sex, her small, button like nipples and her miniature, slightly rough areolas.

The girl gave an inviting smile to Burnham and began to sway her hips to the music. She had a fiery look in her eyes as if daring her audience to partake of her flesh. Her breasts were smaller than the blonde's, coffee cup sized, but were firm and rose high on her chest. Her torso was long and sinuous as she danced. She turned several times, giving a view of her long, back and her round, firm rear globes. When she was sure her body had been properly viewed, she sank to her knees and, spreading her thighs, spread her moist love lips with one hand while she began excitedly frigging her pleasure bud with the other. On her tummy, as on the blonde's, was the angry, black head of the mastiff, Burnham's symbol. It seemed to come alive as her belly undulated. By the time the music stopped, the girl was panting with need, her pale chest flushed pink, her little nipples stiff as darts and a gleam of her pussy's moisture on her fingers. She bowed slightly to her audience and joined the blonde on the side of the room.

There was a moment's silence and then Burnham exclaimed, "Excellent! Very good! Are the others like this?"

"You can be assured," Barouf stated.

"The only problem I see is that the buyers might want to see them all," Burnham said thoughtfully. "But I don't see any way around it. Just do your best to hurry them along. We don't want to make anyone sit in the waiting area for too long."

"As you say, Mr. Burnham," Barouf replied.

The American billionaire took another look at the two beautiful women kneeling expectantly in the room. They were displaying just the right amount of nervousness amidst their lasciviously inviting poses. They had gotten him hot and there was only one real remedy for that.

Burnham rose from his seat. "All in all, very good. Now remember, I know you like to bargain, but everyone should understand before they come into this room that the prices are set. Okay?"

"As you say, Mr. Burnham," Barouf answered. His face was a mask of calmness, but inside he was seething. Who the fuck did these Americans think they are, he thought. "I have been selling pussy for twenty years." But the master of dissemblance gave no indication of his disdain to the American. "And this assistant he gave me," his thoughts continued, "what an eager beaver asshole."

Burnham looked at the two girls as if coming to a decision, which he was. "I'll take the black haired one downstairs for a little while. I want to fuck her," he announced.

"Of course, Mr. Burnham," Barouf replied. Inside he was seething. He didn't want any interference with the girls the day before their sale.

Burnham rose and he gave an indication to the nervous black haired girl to follow him by crooking his finger and wagging it. The girl understood the universal signal at once.

This was too much for Barouf. "No, No, Mr. Burnham!" he exclaimed. "The girl must return the way she came! They are not allowed in the administrative area and she must be bound and gagged to travel! That is the rule!"

Burnham hesitated. He didn't like to be contradicted, but what the old fuck said made sense. "Okay," he said. "But have her down in the guest suite in five minutes."

The guest room was on the second level and Burnham took the elevator down to it. The room was large, about 20' x 30', with a large, four poster bed against one wall. There was a hospitality bar and the American billionaire stepped up to it and poured himself a gin and tonic. A small refrigerator contained some sliced limes and he squeezed one and dropped it into his glass before taking a long, cool, comforting drink. He really didn't have time to spare to dawdle with the random slave girl, but the enticing entertainment he had just seen had made his cock as hard as a brick.

He took the time while waiting for the delivery of the black haired slut to ponder his recent good fortune. If Maddy had not been kidnapped, he would still be in New York working out of the 21st floor of the Chase Manhattan building on 63rd Street. His secretary, Liz, would still be flashing her dazzling 38's at him every day behind her taut sweaters instead of being a tattooed and shaved whore back at his mansion. He would still be forced to pay $2,000 dollar a night hookers to get off, sneaking them up and down the back elevator of his penthouse in the 90's. He wouldn't be getting his dick wet five or six times a day, at least, and he certainly would never have discovered the joy of having a beautiful, defenseless young woman at the business end of a whip.

No, things were going great, better than he could have imagined. The pipeline project was going to produce a profit upwards of 175 million, and that was after everybody was paid off. He had made banking deals with underworld figures around the world, giving the local Ruling Commission a cut, and could guaranty absolute secrecy and security to all kinds of financial transactions. And new slave merchandise was flooding in from all over the place. General Ho had kept his side of the bargain and the Chinese girls were arriving like clockwork. The Latin and South American females were beginning to arrive in a steady flow. And, in a few days, he would receive his first shipment of Southeast Asian girls.

But most of all was the feeling of mastery he got when he surveyed his estate and its environs. He didn't know how many slave girls he owned now. He made a note to have his assistant do an inventory. The feeling of holding literal life and death power over them was wonderfully exhilarating. They knew it too and he reveled in the fear that shone in their eyes every time he called one for service. That was sweet indeed.

And the ponygirls, what could he say about that? He had gotten into the habit of going down to the pony barn at least once a day to pick one out to fuck.

There was only one fly in the ointment. Jake. The ruthless and capable fixer was still honed in on saving Maddy. There would be trouble, he knew that. But he would soon have Maddy. He was sure of that. When the pony, Chocolate, beat her in the match race, Maddy would be his. The problem was that the thought of owning the two premier sulky ponies in the country was more enjoyable than the warm, fuzzy feeling he would get from freeing his niece. He had decided that Maddy would remain Lightning, at least for a couple more years, until she ran herself out. And Chocolate would remain Chocolate, no matter what Jake had promised her. Maddy was already a whore of the worst sort. What had been done to her was unimaginable to him a few short months ago. She had spread her legs and lips for dozens of men, shown her beautiful body to thousands. She was no longer the pretty, saucy, young girl he once knew. If she was, she wouldn't be capable of what she did now, perform spectacular feats as an abject, faceless beast. She was too far gone to save, he believed that firmly. And why should he risk everything that he had done here to save a girl who had refused his offer to send her off to a prestigious college anyway. If she had accepted his offer, she would never have been kidnapped. So it was just as much her fault as anything else.

He had to do something about Jake and he had to be ready to do it by the time the match race was run. Jake would expect Maddy and that whore Jackie to be liberated right away. And there was another reason. If Chocolate lost the match race, he would have to make good on his bet with Grobgy. But what Jake didn't know was that he had not posted mere money against Lightning. He had posted Chocolate. Either he or Grobgy would own the fastest tandem in the sport in a week or two. And if Chocolate lost, Jake would go wild. No, he needed a plan to deal with Jake before Jake dealt with him.

For the time being, though, he needed Jake. He wasn't yet comfortable enough in his position here to do without him. But when he proved himself the great sportsman, winning or losing, his stock would go up immeasurably here in Kalikastan. And then he would be safe.

Burnham's reveries were interrupted by a noise in the corner of the room. There was a cage there, made entirely of clear, luminous Plexiglas. It was about 4' by 4' and had small holes strategically placed around it so that air could get in or out but not interfere with the view of what was inside. It had been empty when he had entered the room, but now a panel slid open in the wall and in crawled the black haired slut who had been dancing for him a few minutes ago.

Her wrists were joined by a short chain that ran through the ring in the back of her collar and she was wearing a shield gag across the lower portion of her face. She emerged from the small entrance, shuffling her knees until she was fully in the little, glass prison. She then knelt in place, her back erect, her elbows lifted upon either side of her head, her knees spread properly widely apart. Her starry blue eyes looked up at him dolefully. His cock gave a little twinge.

Right there before him was all the reason he needed to betray Jake and Maddy both. Her body was delectable and he had already seen an example of her fine training. He couldn't wait to get his lips on her small but firm and plump breasts or his hand between the black trimmed slit between her thighs. And her pale skin looked like it bruised nicely.

He could sense that the girl was apprehensive about her assignment. The man who had been the lord and master of her existence ever since she came to this little vacation spot had bowed and scraped to him like an obsequious servant. She had no idea where she was, had no real idea of what life held in store for her. She had spent the last month or so, although she wouldn't know exactly how long it had been, in the worst hell that she could have imagined. Only through excruciating trial and effort had she earned the opportunity to be free of the horrific tortures that she suffered on the lower floors. And she undoubtedly knew that if she failed to please him in any way, she could be back down there in an instant. She had good reason to be afraid.

Burnham let the girl stew for a few minutes. He went back to the bar and poured himself another drink. He took a long gulp and then began to strip. He didn't want to fuck and run. He wanted to take his sweet time with this slut, a kind of celebration on the success of the training center and of all the good things that had flowed to him in the last seven months.

When he had discarded his coverings, he took another drink and then advanced on the small, glass cage. Barouf was a genius, he had to admit that. Seeing the girl confined and yet exposed to complete view was a turn on. And it was poetic too. For the lessons that the girl had learned in the past few weeks would act as a kind of invisible prison all around her. He had been assured by the psychologists that she would be no more likely to try and escape or shirk her duties than would a fish crawl out of the ocean. It was amazing what a complete and total immersion in a cruel and implacable behavior modification system could do.

The girl, she had been renamed Giselle, as the two inch high letters on her chest denoted, was indeed frightened. She had been told that she was going to be sold. She had known that she was training to be a sexual servant, well, not so much a servant as property. She had even served some of the trainers in this very room, practicing for when she was let back out into the world. But this man was different. He was her master's master. And he looked cruel and demanding. She would have to be at her best, better than her best. If she failed to please him, she would suffer unbearably.

Her thoughts flashed back momentarily to that afternoon back in Lyons. She had taken a break from her early September classes at the university and was lying peaceably on a soft blanket in a rather secluded part of the park. She had been wearing a short skirt and a loose, flowing, short sleeved blouse. It was about 2 in the afternoon and she was lazing in the false summer sun, enjoying the feeling of the heat on her shapely and desirable 22 year old body. She had plans for later, to go out with her boyfriend and dance and drink and fuck. She had wanted to dump him, he was far too possessive for her, but he liked to spend money and he brought her to nice places and so she had decided to wait. He didn't know about the Arab boy she saw on the side. He was for tomorrow night.

A tall, broad shouldered man had emerged from the woods and come upon her. He was good looking and seemed friendly. They sparked up a little conversation. He had a bottle of wine with him and a pair of glasses. He had been stood up, he said and wondered whether she, Marie, would like to share it. She said yes, of course. The man was young and interesting and seemed a lot of fun. Maybe she could dump her boyfriend after all.

The cold, light flavored Chablis went down easily. There was a moment when she all of a sudden got dizzy. The man had not drunk from his glass, but was just sitting there looking at her. She tied to stand, but stumbled. And then the lights went out.

And now she was here, perhaps thousands of miles from Lyons. No one knew where she was. No one would save her. And, as had been confirmed for her more than a hundred times since she had been in this terrible place, she was no longer a college student. She was a whore, a lustful, obedient, servile slut, who would wet herself on command or at the slightest caress. She had no right to refuse any of these men. They had shown her that her role as a pretty, young university student was just a sham. She had been a whore waiting to emerge from the thin veneer of respectability that her culture had imposed. She deserved to be where she was, deserved to be beaten and abused. And if she could please her masters with her body, well, that was the apotheosis of her existence, her only source of joy, her salvation. The men had shown her that.

Burnham stepped up closer to the little, glass booth. There was a little hatch built into the side and he opened it. The girl bent her neck down and crawled out obediently. When she was out, Burnham took hold of the ring in the front of her collar and pulled her to her feet. He ran his sweaty hands over her smooth, pale flesh. It was soft and warm and inviting. He leaned over and took one of her nipples in his mouth and sucked on it gently, relishing the slightly salty taste, the hardness of her teat and the softness which underlay it. She gave out a soft sigh from behind her gag and pressed her bare hips against him. He had his hand on her firm, tight ass and the other on the soft, gracious curve of her hip. He switched breasts, licking and kissing at the nipple, enjoying his mastery over the lovely, young woman. Her belly had caught his thick, hard cock and she was pressing it against his, rotating her hips slightly, exciting his pole with the gentle pressure.

"She's an excellent whore," Burnham thought as he devoured the slight whiff of perfume that her body gave off, mingled with the earthy smell of her flesh. He reached up and released her gag and tossed it on the floor. Grabbing the back of her head, he thrust his tongue into her mouth, mashing his lips against hers. Her tongue greeted his eagerly and she moaned as he played with it, scouring her mouth's hot interior. Her firm breasts were mashed up against his chest and she arched her back, thrusting her pelvis at him.

Burnham decided that he wanted the girl to caress him and so he released her imprisoned wrists and sat down on a plush chair that he dragged out to the middle of the room. He sat on it and spread his legs expectantly. The girl, Giselle, knew just what to do. She brought her body between his strong, heavy thighs and, placing her dainty hands on his chest, began to rub her flesh against his.

Burnham leaned back and closed his eyes, enjoying the friction and heat from her smooth, soft body against his. Her hands wandered around his chest and shoulders and she brought her lips to his neck, kissing it softly and letting her tongue tease it. The hard points of her breasts rubbed across him, up and down as she shifted her positions. She lowered herself and kissed his firm, hard belly as she caressed the inside of his thighs. A few moments later, she dropped her knees to the floor and took hold of his upstanding, rampant cock between her lips.

Her mouth had all the agility of a hand as she played with his stiff tool. She bobbed her head slowly, up and down, while her hands wandered his thighs and stomach. His cock pierced the edge of her throat and Burnham groaned at the sensation of entering that tight, hot zone. She moaned and sighed lustfully as she worked, bringing Burnham aural as well as physical pleasure.

When his cock became ready to explode, the black haired slave girl relented her amorous attentions to it and resumed kissing and exploring Burnham's excited body. The second time she taunted his excited flesh was even better than the first as his need for completion idled at the base of his cock. The girl captured his iron rod between her graceful, thin thighs and slid her moist, hot pussy across it, transferring to him some of her leaking fluids. She did that three or four times, making Burnham grasp his hands into large, tense fists so as to prevent the explosion of his cock. And then she released him and started the process all over, kissing his neck and shoulders and all the way down his torso until she had captured his long, hard pole once more between her lips.

Burnham reveled in the girl's exquisite pleasuring of his body. He decided that he wanted to penetrate her and so he took hold of her arms and stood from his chair. His cock was so enflamed with need that it throbbed as he led her to the bed. He pushed her down on it and lay down next to her. He wanted to cool off before he fucked her, making the pleasure of using her last. She was on her back and he next to her and he glided his strong but soft hands down her long, curvaceous frame, running it up and down, over her breasts and belly. She moaned and squirmed with her own need as he caressed her. Her eyes looked dutifully at his, waiting for any signal that he might give as to his desires.

Staring down at the girl's taut, but soft belly, Burnham appreciated his mark of ownership on her, the fierce, terrorizing, black dog with its reddened teeth and piercing red eyes. It looked like it had just been interrupted from a feast on some poor creature's freshly killed flesh. It was an indelible mark of her enslavement. The slave trade was just a sideline to him. The earnings from the whorehouses that he had started up in the capital and at the pipeline work camps were just chicken feed compared to his other endeavors. But it gave him an immense sense of pride and power to see his symbol etched on the women's flesh, knowing that they lived at his discretion, served at his whim, performed the functions that he detailed for them. And better yet, that in the mansions and pied-à-terres of the wealthy and powerful of the country, men of power and influence would see his totem, the symbol of his wealth and power as their whores lay back and spread their legs for them.

The callous billionaire took hold of the soft, engorged lips between the young girl's thighs. Her black pubic hair had been reduced to little more than bristles on each side of it and the feel of the short, stiff hairs on his palm was exciting. The girl had her knees up and her legs spread wide invitingly and she moaned with pleasure as he caressed her cunt, fingering the hard button at its top, thrusting his digits inside her. Satisfied with exploring the soft, yielding flesh of her front, Burnham urged the girl to her belly. She turned obediently and sighed as she stroked her long, narrow back and caressed the firm, round globes of her rear.

Ready to make his penetration of her flesh, Burnham pulled the black haired slave girl to her knees and raised her ass. He took a position behind her and pressed her soft, graceful thighs wider with his hands as he presented his stiff cock to her dilated, leaking canal. He probed it with his prick's meaty head and then slid himself inside, sighing heavily as the warm heat surrounded his pole. Her cunt was tight and agile and he could feel her muscles clasp him as he rode back and forth within her cavity. His hands were on her hips holding her steady as he rocked his hips. She was bent over, her breasts crushed against her knees, her braceleted hands clamped close to her body. She moaned with pleasure as he rode her, shuddering several times as he dragged his pole against her stiffened love bud.

Not satisfied with plowing the girl's steamy cleft, Burnham withdrew himself abruptly and addressed himself to the tiny brown star between her proffered rear cheeks. Her moisture was clinging to his rod and he was able to easily spread the small, brown ring and plunge within her. She gave a groan and her body shook as she experienced her first orgasm at her lord's hands. She called out her pleasure to the room, "Ohhhhhhh! Ohhhhhhh! Ohhhhhhh!" as the thrill of his possession of her spread throughout her body.

The men had made her like this. They had ravaged the small hole again and again, stroking her fevered slash as they did so, whipping her unmercifully when she failed to respond. Now the feel of a thick cock in her bowels, the rasping of a cock along the sensitive tissue of the tiny, brown tinted opening, drove her lusts.

Burnham reached his hands around the girl's torso and seized hold of her breasts. She raised her head automatically to give him better access. But it was not the gentle, passionate caresses that the man had heretofore given them that she received. Burnham squeezed his large, strong hands together, mauling her mounds until she moaned with pain. The man had no interest in her pleasure. Sure, it was fun to watch a slut moaning and twisting in pleasure as you fucked her, but Burnham was concerned principally now with the assuagement of his lusts and passions. He wanted to hear the girl whine and moan with pain. He took hold of her little nipples and twisted them so hard that her torso seemed to contract and her cry of anguish filled the room. Just the sound of it made his cock thrill with pleasure.

Not satisfied to abuse the girl's mounds, Burnham forced her to come erect on her knees so that he could access her delicate, hot pussy. He reached around her hip as he continued to thrust himself up into her and took the blood engorged folds between his fingers and clamped them shut. She bent her head down as she absorbed the pain all the while not forgetting to use the muscles of her small opening to accentuate her abuser's pleasure. "Ohhhhhhhh!" she moaned as the pain intensified. "Ohhhhhhhh!"

Burnham moved his fingers upwards and took hold of her rigid clit. Capturing it between his thumb and his forefinger, he squeezed it until the girl cried out, "Oh! Oh! Ohhhhhhh!"

The sound of the girl's unhappy cries triggered his climax and his cock began to jet its stream of viscous, white fluids into the girl's depths. Burnham groaned as the pleasure of his ejaculations jolted him again and again. His brain fogged with the waves of delight sent to it by his throbbing cock. As his orgasm waned, he gave the girl's now bruised clit one more, hearty squeeze. She cried out in agony, bringing added enjoyment to his last, few, waning spasms.

The satisfied slaver pushed the girl's torso back down and leaned himself over her as he recovered his sensibilities. "Oh, that was good," he thought languidly. "She's an excellent toy."

Once his shrinking cock slipped fee of he girl's ass, Burnham rose from the bed. The slave girl obediently remained as she was. He could hear her sniffles of self pity as he stepped over to a small wash basin and cleaned off his soiled pole. When he was done, he dressed quickly. He wasn't done with this cunt. He wanted to watch her and hear her scream as he whipped her. But not now. He had to get back to the mansion. There were deals to massage, decisions to make, things to arrange. He had better talk to his security chief, Boradin about Jake, he thought.

Satisfied at his pleasurable interlude, Burnham opened a small closet in the bedroom and found a six foot long steel leash. After ordering the girl to her feet, he locked her hands behind her and thrust her gag back between her still trembling lips.

As she felt her wrists joined behind her and the thick, leather gag slide over her tongue, its shield sealing her lips behind them, the girl wondered miserably, "Is this what it will be like as a slave girl? Will all of the men hurt me like this? How much will I have to bear? And for how long?"

Burnham saw the tears flowing down the girl's face. "I guess she expected something different," he thought. "Well I better disabuse her of that at once." He hated it when they cried afterwards. Maybe the girl wasn't as well trained as she seemed?

The big American pushed the girl back down on the bed. He raised her legs until her ankles were almost to her neck. He had picked up the short chain that had previously bound the girl's wrists behind her head and he connected the bracelets on her ankles, running the chain through the ring in the front of her collar.

The girl looked up at him unhappily. She knew that he had not made her assume this position for no reason. She watched as he returned to the closet where he had gotten the leash and when he returned she saw that he had a three foot long lash in his hand. She closed her eyes and moaned with dismal anticipation.

Burnham forwent any preliminaries. He struck the inside of the girl's right thigh with a mighty blow of the whip, making her body jump and her legs tremble. She screamed behind her sealed lips as she received the intense, fiery message of pain. Tears were now flowing freely down her face. She bit down on the stifling gag in an attempt to accept stoically the next red hot bite of the lash, but when it landed, she released another long, woeful wail. Her ankles pulled desperately at the chain that bound them up over her chest.

Burnham worked his way up and down the girl's thighs with enthusiasm. His cock had hardened again at the sight of the girl's suffering. Long, red stripes had appeared on her flesh where the lash had landed. It was visually exciting to see the stark contrast between her pale flesh and the long, maroon trails.

The cruel man centered himself between the girl's upraised thighs and brought the whip down hard on her still moist and engorged mound. Her voice was growing harsh with her cries of agony. He struck the soft, tender opening twice more, sending the girl into a paroxysm of pain.

The billionaire's blood was boiling once again. He had no time to undress, and so he fished his cock out of his pants and stood between the girl's upraised legs. He plunged himself inside her, making her moan and whine as her abused flesh suffered the impact of his cock. Holding the girl's ankles firmly in his hands, he thrust himself along her tortured crevasse until he felt his passion rising. His cock quickly burst into another series of ecstatic throbs and jerks inside the girl's damaged pussy. He groaned and his eyes rolled back as he received the pleasure.

Now he was done. He stood back and returned his meaty weapon to his pants and zipped himself up. He had changed his mind. It wasn't that the girl was insufficiently trained. It was just the opposite. They had taught her pain without taking away her fear and dread of it. If anything, they had heightened her reactivity to create a creature that could receive an endless series of blows day after day and still would genuinely and satisfyingly wail and cry as she was tormented. She was as close to a perfect slave girl as you could get. He made a note to complement Barouf and the professors when he next saw them.

Burnham released the girl's ankles and pulled her to her feet. She swayed unsteadily, looking at him with a new sense of fear. She followed his lead dolefully as he led her from the room.

"I'm taking this one with me," Burnham explained to the man at the front desk as he pulled the unfortunate girl behind him through the door to the outside. He led her down the five steps to ground level and over to where his big, white skinned ponygirls were waiting for him. He attached the leash to the rear of the cart and hopped up. He gave a crack of the reins and the ponies jumped into action.

Amidst her sorrow and unhappiness, the girl took note of her surroundings as she emerged into the outer world for the first time since her arrival at this modern, smartly designed hell hole. She blinked in wonderment when she saw the two large, naked, big breasted women hitched to the cart. The sight of the bizarrely outfitted women, hoods over their heads, bits through their mouths, was shocking. She had thought that she was now fully inured to the cruelties of the men who had taken her by force from her far away home. But, she realized, she had no real idea of the measure of the cruelties that these men were capable of. She felt a knot grow in her stomach as her leash was tied off to the rear of the cart. When the small vehicle began to move forward, propelling the naked, bound and gagged slave girl helplessly behind it, she gave out a deep, heartfelt sob.

CHAPTER FIVE
LIFE'S HARD LESSONS

Jackie, the brown skinned ponygirl now known as Chocolate, lay inside her ponygirl trailer, her ankles bound together and fixed to the floor, her eyelets on her hood closed. The rain was pelting down on the tin roof of the small structure like a thousand little drummer boys. She was lying on her bound arms and her collar had been tied off to the rings on the trailer floor. A broad strap circled her muscular thighs, keeping her legs bound tightly together. Her mouth was gagged, with a leather shield across her lower face and a thick, long, leather probe in her mouth. It had been this way every night since she had become a ponygirl. She was used to it, but every once in a while, during her nights of fitful sleep, when her dreams turned to when she had been a woman, her body would shift in her bonds and she would awaken, terrified and distraught until she remembered where she was and what she had become.

She had been dreaming of when she was a teenager, before all of the bad things that had occurred in her life had happened. She was a star miler at her high school in the Southside of Chicago. She had lost the State Championship by two one hundredths of a second. In her dream she was running a race around the circular track in the stadium where she had won the Chicago All High School Mile Race. She had started out running intently, edging ahead of the other girls. It was a sunny and bright, midafternoon. The crowd was cheering and she felt exhilarated by the noise and the idea that everyone was watching her cruise to victory. But, then, the stadium began to darken. The yells of the crowd became taunting jeers. She looked around and the girls she had been running with had all disappeared. Out of the darkness behind her came a huge, black hand. It was outstretched and she knew that it was reaching to seize her. She turned away and began to pump her legs furiously, desperate to escape it. She could feel it coming closer and closer and she tried to scream, but her voice was muffled and nothing came out but an anguished moan. The track had turned to mud and her feet seemed mired in the gelatinous substance. As the hand began to clasp around her, she tried to raise her hands to ward it off, but they were stuck in place and she could not move them. Suddenly, the hand closed around her body. She tried to scream again as she felt it bind her body, her legs and torso, immobilizing her. And then she woke up.

The first thing that she saw was the utter darkness behind her black, Neoprene ponygirl hood. She twisted and writhed her body and tried to raise her head. But she was firmly bound into a cruel stasis. She moaned and struggled, straining her muscles, her heart beating wildly. She could feel a thick, long intruder in her mouth and she tried to push it out, ramming her tongue up against it futilely.

When the distraught ponygirl finally realized where she was and that she had just emerged from a terrible dream, she broke out into sobs. The feeling of powerlessness in her dream had been terrible and now she had awoken to discover that it was true. She flexed her powerful, bound thighs and pulled frantically on the leather thongs that kept her ankles extended and fixed to the ground. She tried to sit up, but the chains to her collar held her in place. Convinced of the futility of her efforts, she gave a moan of unhappiness and let her sickened body relax.

Life had been hard for Jackie. Not at first, though. She had had a regular family, with a father and mother who loved her, a sister and three brothers. Her parents had worked hard to make her and her siblings a good home. They had never wanted for anything really important. But when she was fifteen, her brother, Johnny, had been killed in a drive by one night outside of their simple, but well kept house. Johnny had not been a gang member, but the friend who had been standing next to him was. The bullet missed its intended target and struck Johnny right in the chest.

Things started to go downhill after that. Her mother never fully recovered and Jackie would often hear her at night in her bedroom crying over her lost boy. Her father, a deacon in their church, had started drinking and became morose and violent. Her older sister, Louise, got out as soon as she finished high school and moved away to Los Angeles, to get in the movies, she said. No one had heard from her for many months, but someone had said that they saw her dancing in a titty bar just off of the Strip. Her brothers Luke and Andrew both joined the Marines and she guessed that they were doing okay, but they rarely wrote home and spent their infrequent leaves with their friends.

And so, Jackie had been lonely when, at 17, she met the sharply dressed, older, fast talking, young man from across town. He was handsome and well built, perhaps 26 or 27 years old, black as coal, and he had lots of money, or so it seemed. The other girls told her that he was no good, but he always treated her with respect and kindness. Jackie didn't dare tell her father or mother about him; she knew that they would disapprove. His name was Alphonse, but everybody called him Taquan.

She had given Taquan her virginity in a sleazy motel one night. After that, they made love regularly, or as often as she saw him. He would meet her on her way home from school and drive her off to the motel in his big. flashy car. Sometimes, he would take her to night clubs where, since she was underage, he would slip a twenty to the door man who would let her in with a big, lugubrious smile.

It was heaven to the unhappy, lonely girl to be in the man's strong arms. He taught her to please him with her mouth and he made her scream with passion as he licked her between her thighs. She had long, well toned legs from track and he liked to run his strong, black hands along her coffee colored flesh. Sometimes she did not see him for a week or two. He had no telephone number that she knew of and he would make their assignations with her from the driver's seat of his shiny, black Mercedes when she saw him parked on her route from her school back to her house or, sometimes, in the mornings on her way to class.

One night, she met him on the corner about three blocks from her house. She had told her mother she was going to a girlfriend's. Jackie knew that the grief distracted woman would never check. Instead of taking her to the motel, which she had expected, they drove around while he explained how much trouble he was in. It seemed that he owed a small fortune to a gambler and the guy had threatened to kill him. She had never seen Taquan so upset. She was almost in tears at the thought of harm coming to him.

And then came the pitch. In any con, there's the setup and then the pitch. You get the mark all worked up and then lower the boom. Maybe, at first, not a big one, but enough so that he or she is on an unalterable road to disaster.

Taquan explained tearfully that this guy had seen him with her and wanted to have a date. He just wanted to take her out and show her off, that's all. She wouldn't have to do anything. Just be pretty and nice to the man. He would forgive part of Taquan's debt and give him more time to pay the rest. Jackie was shocked at the suggestion, but at Taquan's assurance that all she would have to do was smile and be polite, she said okay. After all, it was the least that she could do for the man who had brought her so much warmth and love.

The man turned out to be in his fifties. He had a broad, heavy face and a belly as big as a base drum. He was dressed in flashy clothes and wore a stylish, brown fedora with a red silk ribbon around it. Taquan introduced him as Leo. He was driving a shiny, black Cadillac. His big, meaty hand shook hers gently and he had a disarming smile. Jackie looked nervously back at Taquan before she got into the man's car, but his face was reassuring and grateful.

Leo took Jackie to a club up on the North Side. She was wearing one of the pretty, short skirts that she had bought from the money that Taquan had been giving her and a revealing, silk blouse. Jackie had large breasts, even when she was younger. She had turned eighteen a couple of weeks ago and her feminine beauty was in full bloom. She had shiny, smooth, graceful thighs and a noble face. She was tall and a bit broad shouldered and heavy limbed, but her torso had a graceful curve to it and the combination of her body's assets made her look beautifully statuesque. Her jet black hair was silky and long. She had made herself especially pretty for Taquan tonight since she hadn't seen him in a couple of weeks.

The man chatted amiably with Jackie as they rode through the dirty, Chicago, night streets. He kept looking at her breasts and her appealing thighs. "That's okay," Jackie thought. "So long as he doesn't touch me." He took her to a noisy nightclub filled with happy, well dressed people.

The night went by quickly. Leo didn't dance, but a couple of men came up to him during the night and received permission to take the tall, lovely, young girl who was with him onto the dance floor. Jackie danced with delight and was a little sorry when Leo announced that it was time to go.

Jackie was surprised when Leo pulled the car down a dark, dead end street. She had no idea where they were and the area around them looked bombed out. The street lights had been broken, there was garbage strewn all over the street and sidewalks and a high, chain link fence surrounding a ragged, weedy, overgrown lot. The still naïve girl became nervous when Leo turned off the car's engines and doused the lights.

The fat man pulled a flask of bourbon from his large, oversized suit jacket and took a long gulp. He offered some to Jackie, who declined. She had started to drink when Taquan took her out, but usually had a wine spritzer or a rum and coke, but never more than one or two. Tonight she had had three rum and cokes and they seemed stronger than the ones she was used to drinking. Her head was light and her body felt funny. She watched the big man nervously as he put the flask away in his pocket.

"So," the man said in his deep, base toned voice, "Taquan told you to be nice to me, right?"

Jackie nodded her head, afraid of what the man was referring to.

"Well," the man continued, drinking her up with his large, bulbous eyes, "this is the time when you get to be nice to me. Understand?"

"N,no," Jackie said hesitatingly. "Taquan said…"

"Taquan said you have to be nice to me, bitch!" the man said angrily. "What did you think he meant! Do you think I took you out and showed you a good time so that we could shake hands and say goodnight?"

Jackie was trembling. She had never been so frightened in her life. She tried to answer the man's hostile question, but her voice wouldn't come out.

The man reached over to her with his big right arm and placed it on her naked thigh. "Come on honey," he said sweetly now. "I just want a little blow job. That's all. You're so pretty and you got me all hot. Just suck me off and I'll take you home, okay?"

The thought of putting the man's dick in her mouth made Jackie swoon with nausea. "I, I don't want to," she said miserably.

"Listen bitch," the man said harshly, "if you don't put out for me, the deal's off with Taquan. Tomorrow, I'll have some of my home boys track him down and put a cap into him. Is that what you want?"

The frightened eighteen year old started to cry. No, that wasn't what she wanted. She loved Taquan. Maybe she should do what the man wanted. Just this once. She was afraid of what he would do to her if she continued to refuse, too. It was lonely and dark outside. She didn't have any money and she was a long, long way from her house.

The man's fat hand gave Jackie's thigh a painful squeeze as if to emphasize her peril and his power over her. She looked at him dolefully. He was at least three times bigger than her. She could open the door next to her and run. There wasn't a fat man in the world who could catch her. But where would she go? She could be raped or robbed or murdered.

Tears were streaming down her face as Jackie nodded her assent. She would do anything to get out of this mess. She had sucked Taquan's cock many times and that had been okay. How much worse could it be to suck Leo's? It would be over in a few minutes and then she would never have to see the man again. And she would have saved Taquan.

The man smiled a toothy grin at the girl's assent. He pressed the lever that made the steering wheel go up and then made the seat go all the way back. He tilted it back so that he was relaxed and then opened his fly. His thick, black cock was already hard and it sprung up like a snake popping out of a hole. He lifted his right leg so that it was stretched along the front seat. Jackie had to shift as his shiny, black, pointed shoe nudged into place behind her.

"Okay, girl," he said. "Let's get to it."

Jackie suppressed a sob as she crawled over the seat so that she could have access to the man's lap. She put one knee between the man's fat legs and one foot on the floor of the car over his large thigh to balance herself. As she leaned over, she pushed her long black hair behind her ears. The snake like tube of flesh stared up at her.

"Come on, bitch," the man spat out churlishly. "I ain't got all night!"

Jackie's stomach churned as she gingerly surrounded the man's dark meat with her lips. She pressed her head down like Taquan had taught her and let it slide over her tongue. Its presence in her mouth was like an evil, monstrous thing. Her whole being revolted at the salty taste and the smell of the man's loins. It was like the whole world outside had disappeared into the small confines of the man's stylish car and that her entire being was now centered around the offensive presence in her mouth.

Jackie heard the man groan as she eased her lips down his stiffened pole. It was fatter and longer than Taquan's cock and she choked a little bit as it reached the edge of her throat. She decided that she needed to get this over with as soon as possible. She began to bob her head up and down quickly hoping that the man's prick would explode. But she felt his strong, fat hand take hold of her hair and bring her actions to a forced halt.

"Whoa, bitch!" the man exclaimed. "Take your time. Pretend that you like it."

With a sob, Jackie began to slowly and languorously stroke the man's cock with her mouth. His hand guided her up and down gently but firmly. Her stomach was churning and her heart was beating wildly. Her hands were resting gingerly on the man's fat thighs as if mere contact with his body would soil her.

The heat was building up in the interior of the car. The only sounds were the man's soft sighs and the slurping of her lips on his cock. The man circled his free hand under her chest and grabbed one of her breasts and squeezed it.

Jackie gave out a whine of dismay and tried to rise from her task to protest. But the man held her head firmly in place.

"You've got great tits, bitch," he told her as he mangled her breast with his hand. "I want you to unbutton your blouse so I can feel them."

Jackie tried to shake her head no, but the man grabbed her hair even more tightly and shook it viciously.

"Don't tell me no, cunt! I want to feel your tits! So do what I say or I'll throw you out of the car right here and go see your boyfriend tomorrow!"

The distraught girl nodded her head as best as she was able in unhappy consent. She tried to rise up so that she could comply with the man's demand but he held her face married to his lap.

"Don't get up, stupid," he said. "Just loosen the buttons."

Crying with dismal dismay, Jackie placed her weight on her knees and raised her hands from the man's thighs. Unhappily, the man's meat still plugging her mouth, her hands trembling, she loosened the buttons one by one until her blouse hung free and open. She was wearing a lacy, mauve half brassiere that covered just the bottom portions of her breasts up to the nipples. The man's heavy hand pushed the delicate fabric aside and freed her right mound. She felt it burst out of its enclosure and the heat of the man's sweaty palm engulf it. She moaned with misery as he squeezed and probed it. She dolefully resumed the caresses of his cock with her mouth and he began to groan and moan with pleasure. His hips were rocking to meet her and his grip had resumed its firmness on her hair. Suddenly, his cock exploded and a swell of his warm, viscous spewm flooded her mouth. As he came, he squeezed her breast harshly, making her moan with pain. She choked and coughed as she tried to let his tart tasting cum out, but the man shook her head viciously and demanded, "Swallow it, cunt! If you spit it out I'll whup you good!"

Dismayed and frightened, Jackie let the slimy fluids slip down her throat.

Afterwards, the man was all smiles and pleasantries. "You good enough," he said. "You could use a little more practice, honey, but you'll do." He laughed at his joke. Jackie was leaning back in the corner of the car as far away from the man as she could get. She had tucked her breast back in her bra and was remorsefully buttoning her shiny, silken blouse. One of the buttons had come off.

Leo removed his flask from his pocket again and took a long drink. He proffered it to the tearful, shamed girl. This time she took it.

When Leo dropped her off to where Taquan had agreed to meet them, Jackie was silent and morose. Taquan took no notice. He drove the car to one of their spots and he pulled her towards him and kissed her. "Thank you, baby. You're the best. It wasn't too bad, was it?"

Jackie did not know whether she should tell Taquan about the blow job. She was afraid that he would get mad and not see her again. On the other hand, she thought, maybe he knew all along. He was the one who told her to be nice to the man. But as he put his lips on hers and his tongue entered her mouth all that was forgotten. She had helped the man she loved. He didn't need to know what she had to do. If he knew that she had blown the fat man, would he be kissing her soiled lips now?

Taquan lowered the seats to the big, black Mercedes and pushed Jackie's short skirt up to her waist. She lifted her hips as he drew her panties over her hips. He then dragged them down her long, graceful, fit thighs and over her knees. She happily lifted her feet one by one as he drew them over her red sparkled high heels. When his cock penetrated her, Jackie moaned with pleasure. She had saved the man that she loved and he was thanking her by making sweet love to her. He made her orgasm twice before he spilled himself within her.

Jackie and Taquan went out a few more times before the issue of Leo came up again. She had assured him more than once that she had had a good time and that nothing bad had happened. He didn't need to know, she thought. She promised to keep her secret locked deep inside her.

She gave out a soft sob when, one night about two weeks later, Taquan's Mercedes pulled up next to Leo's Caddy. She had thought that she had seen the last of the dastardly fat man.

"Come on, Jackie," Taquan insisted when she demurred about going with the man again. "I need you to do this. I still owe Leo a lot of money. It's not like its anything bad. Just go with him, have a few drinks, dance, and I'll see you a little later."

Jackie was torn. She had lied to Taquan and didn't want him to know. But on the other hand, if she went with Leo, he'd demand another blow job. She started to cry.

"What's the matter, Jackie," Taquan asked impatiently. "Shit, all I ask is that you go out with a friend for a little while and you give me the big boo hoo thing. Do you want him to mess me all up?"

"He's not your friend," Jackie squalled. "How can he be your friend if he wants to hurt you?"

"You don't understand anything, Jackie," Taquan returned to her. "It's business. If word got around town that I stiffed him, he'd have all kind of trouble collecting from anyone else. As long as I can keep him happy, everything's all right. He'll only get mad if I welsh. Please, baby. You've got to help me."

Jackie reluctantly got out of the car. Before she left, Taquan gave her a big kiss and gave her breast a gentle caress. "Later honey, I'll give you some more of daddy's good stuff."

Leo didn't wait until after the nightclub to pull over and demand Jackie's services. She blew him quickly and cleanly without argument, hoping that that would mean that he wouldn't demand another on the way home. She was subdued and depressed when they got to the club. When Leo stopped the car, he reached under the seat and pulled out a small mirror. He went into his pocket and removed a small bag of white powder. He shook some out and then deftly chopped it up with a credit card, arranging it into two long lines on the shiny, reflective surface. He rolled up a $100 bill and snorted one line down quickly.

"Ahhhhhhh," he sighed as the drug entered his brain. "Just what the doctor ordered. Here," he said, proffering the C note to Jackie. "You do the other one."

Jackie shook her head. "No way," she thought. She was still running track and didn't want to fail a drug test at school. They gave them randomly to the athletes. She had had one in the fall, but no one had been asked since. But what was the sense of taking chances?

"Come on, baby," Leo said. "It'll make you feel real good. I don't want you moping around all night."

Jackie looked at the white powder on the mirror. It looked so harmless and she was so unhappy. Maybe just this once. It would make being with the offensive man all night more tolerable.

Jackie nodded and then leaned over. She was unable to get the whole line in before her head started to seem like it was swelling and her body began to tingle all over. "Wow!" she thought. "Oh my god!"

She sat up and shook her head.

"Good stuff, eh, baby?" Leo asked happily. "Come on, finish it up and we'll go inside."

Jackie had the time of her life in the bar. She laughed and danced with Leo's friends. She drank five rum and cokes, but it didn't seem to have any effect on her. She was sweaty and happy when Leo said that it was time to go. Like the last time, she was sorry to leave, but even more so. She was having a good time.

On the way home, Leo pulled the Caddy down the same empty, demolished street. Jackie knew what he wanted. It was okay. She would do it and then she would go see Taquan. He would make it all all right. He had promised her some delight and she was looking forward to it.

Leo pulled out the mirror and they both did a little line. This time, he ordered her to remove her blouse and bra before she blew him. Jackie hesitated and, to her surprise, Leo slapped her. "Do what I say, bitch," he demanded.

Tearfully, her head confused and wooly, Jackie complied. She slowly and, this time, carefully, unbuttoned her blouse and laid it on the back of the seat. She reached behind her and unhooked her bra. Leo's eyes were drinking her up. She hesitated briefly, ashamed at showing her beauties to the cruel, offensive man.

"Come on, come on," Leo said impatiently. "Let me see 'em."

Jackie gave her shoulders a little shrug and the straps of her bra fell down her upper arms. With another practiced motion, it slid down her arms and she pulled it over her sweaty hands. She could feel her breasts sway as she moved her torso. Her nipples were hard with fear and shame. She draped the small, lacy garment over her blouse and turned back to her tormentor.

Her round, firm, full breasts swung freely as she moved. Leo took hold of them and squeezed and played with the heavy orbs. "Now those are nice tits, baby," he said lugubriously. "It's a shame to hide them. I could play with them all night long." He tweaked her stiffened nipples and then told her to get to work.

Jackie knelt over and started to suck on Leo's cock. Her mind was swimming with the drugs and the alcohol. There was something thrilling, despite her shame, at being half naked in the man's car and sucking his dick, hearing the big man moan and sigh in pleasure. His hands were massaging her breasts as she worked on him. His fat fingers were strong and from time to time she moaned as his grip on her mammaries became too hard. She had been at it for about ten minutes, doing it nice and slow as he had demanded, when she felt Leo's big hand pull at her hair until she was kneeling up. His fat cock plopped out of her surprised mouth.

"I want to suck on your tits, honey," the man explained. He pulled her torso towards him and subsumed first one nipple and then the other between his fat lips. Jackie tried to push herself away from him, but he was too strong for her. Her body felt insulted even as the man's big lips excited her. He sucked long and steady on them, one after the other, until Jackie, unwillingly, moaned with pleasure. She was ashamed as soon as she did it. What would Taquan think? How could she ever tell him?

The aroused eighteen year old was surprised when the fat man shoved her back. "Take off your panties, baby," he said. "I want to fuck you."

Jackie was shocked and frightened at the man's churlish demand. "P,please," she said, her lips trembling and an empty place opening in her tummy. "Please don't make me," she said again, starting to cry.

The big man took a hold of her stiffened, wet nipples and twisted them harshly. "If you don't take off your panties and lie back, I'll really fuck you up, you stupid cunt!" he said angrily.

Jackie moaned as the pain shot through her. No one had ever done this to her before. She hadn't been aware that pinching her nipples could hurt so much. "Okay, okay," she said plaintively. "I'll do it, please let go! Please!"

"Okay, then," the man said as he released her teats. Crying and sobbing, the unhappy girl leaned back and reached under her pretty, short skirt. She pulled her panties over her hips and drew them over her feet. Leo pulled a lever and the front seat fell back. He grabbed her by her shoulders and forced her back on the now flat surface. He shifted his huge body until he was between her legs and then lifted her ankles until her high heeled shoes scraped the roof. He looked down at her furry bush. "Mmmm-mmmmmm, baby!" he said licking his fat lips. "You got one hot pussy! No wonder Taquan likes you so much!"

At the mention of her lover's name, Jackie began to cry again. "What would Taquan say if he knew?" she thought miserably. It was too late to try and get away. If she struggled, the man would just slap and hurt her again. The man joined her ankles above her and held them in one, large, forceful hand while he held his fat cock in his free hand and probed at her loins. She felt the round head locate her slit and push inside her. She groaned in misery as she felt it side up her slick channel.

"You're all wet, baby," Leo said mockingly. "You're a natural born whore." He pushed himself the rest of the way inside her until his fat belly touched against her stomach.

The worst part of it was that Jackie did not know what to do with her hands. She didn't want to touch the cruel man as he pumped his cock back and forth inside her. She wanted to try and push him off, but she knew that any such feeble attempt was doomed to failure and likely to prompt the man's hair trigger temper. Finally, she crooked her right arm over her eyes so that she would not have to see him as he pleasured himself within her. She wrapped her left arm across her body, over her breasts, to stop them from jumping and swaying as her body received the force of the man's powerful thrusts.

"Oooooou, baby! Ooooooouuuu, baby!" he kept saying as he stroked himself along the course of her flooded crevasse. Jackie moaned with unhappiness as she felt her tender clit rubbed again and again by the top of his long, fat pole, making her passions rise unwillingly. She didn't want to come for this mean, conscienceless man. That was for Taquan, and him only.

When she felt the man's cock begin to throb and jerk inside her, she was happy. It was almost over. Leo grunted and groaned as he got himself off. "Ooouuuu, baby! Ooooouuuu, baby!" he repeated again and again.

Leo gave a great sigh and his body relaxed. He leaned his heavy body against her distended thighs, pushing them down and keeping her ankles in his iron like grip. His face was inches away from hers. "You're one hot fuck!" he told her delightedly. "Your cunt is nice and tight! I could fuck you every night of the week!"

Jackie moaned in misery at the very thought of fucking the callous man again. She expected him to let her rise now. He had gotten what he wanted, hadn't he? But when she felt his cock resume its slide back and forth in her squishy canal, flooded by the comingling of his discharge and her involuntary moisture, she realized that he was still hard. He was going to do it again!

"Please, don't!" Jackie moaned as his cock began another search for completion. "Pleeeeeease!"

"Oh, baby, you know you like it," Leo said tauntingly. "Your pussy's all wet and hot, so shut the fuck up!"

Leo huffed and puffed as he plowed her cleft for the second time. This time, he fucked her long and slow. She could feel his cock glide along her hot canal back and forth in a languorous, relaxed rhythm. He made a special effort to rasp it along her hardened clit. Jackie felt her lust rising and her mind revolted at what the man was doing to her. She tried to rise, but the pressure of the man's body against her upraised thighs kept her pinned to the seat. "Oh, god, please stop, please, please!" she cried out as she felt her lusts begin to build. "Don't make me come, please, please!"

Leo gave out a hearty, demonic laugh. "Come for me, baby!" he mocked her. "Come for Daddy!"

Jackie clenched her useless fists and crooked both of her arms over her head. "Oooooooooh!" she moaned as her cunt began to shudder with preorgasmic delight. "No, please, noooooooo! Ahhhhhhh! Ahhhhhhhhh! Ahhhhh-hhhhh!" she screamed as the contractions of her fevered tunnel sent waves of pleasure through her. "Ahhhhhhhh! Ahhhhhhhh!" she called out, her voice filling the small enclosure.

"Yeah, baby!" Leo called out. "You're so fucking hot, I can't believe it! Go, baby, go!"

Jackie was still coming when she felt the man's body stiffen and heard him groan. "Ahhhhhhhhhh!" he yelled. "Yeah! Yeah!"

When Leo had stopped jetting his cum inside of her, he released her ankles and fell back into the driver's seat. "You're good, honey," he said as he pulled out the flask of bourbon that he always kept handy.

Jackie just lay there, moaning in unhappiness. "How did I get into this?" she thought miserably. "What will I tell Taquan?"

But she wouldn't tell Taquan anything. He would never understand. Leo ordered her to dress and, "…quit the bawling." He kept her underwear.

"Please give it back to me," she asked him timidly.

"No way, baby. This stuff's going in the Hall of Fame," he answered her, laughing. "Here, have a drink."

The unhappy girl took a long sip of the bourbon. When she had it tilted back to her lips, Leo put his hand on the bottom and raised it, causing it to rush into her mouth. It flowed down her throat, burning and she coughed and gagged. It spilled on her blouse, causing a dark, wet spot. She tried to move her head away and she reached out for the man's strong hand, but he merely placed his other hand around her cheeks and, after letting catch her breath, forced more of the intoxicating liquor into her.

Jackie's brain was numb as the man circled the top back on the bottle and put it back in his pocket. "Feel better?" he asked her smiling.

The girl merely turned her face away from him and scrunched up next to the door.

She felt sick to her stomach when Leo dropped her off where Taquan said he would meet them. She got into Taquan's car, trying not to cry. Again, her lover seemed not to sense anything wrong. She remembered that he had promised her some of his "sweet stuff" tonight and she was hoping at all costs to avoid it. She didn't want Taquan to notice that she had no underwear on. And she didn't want his cock to ply the same path that Leo had until she had cleaned herself and gotten the feel of his prick out of her pussy. But Taquan took her to their spot again.

"I'm not feeling too good," she said to her boyfriend meekly. He looked at her with anger.

"Man, I've been waiting here for you all night and you've been out dancing and shit, and you're going to tell me no?"

"I'm just not feeling that good, honey," she said weakly. "I'm sorry."

"Jeeeeze," Taquan said. "I can't believe it. I don't know when I'm going to get to see you again, cause I'm going to be busy. You want me to fuck some other girl? Is that what I have to do?"

"No, baby," Jackie replied. "I don't want you to do that. Maybe tomorrow...."

"No tomorrow, bitch!" he spat out at her. "And no next day either. After all the things I've done for you and all the stuff I've given you, money and presents, you're going to pull this on me? What's the matter, did you get all the loving you need tonight from Leo? Are you fucking him?"

A gulf opened in Jackie's belly. Did he know? "No, sweetie!" she protested. "Nothing like that, honest!"

Taquan leaned back in his seat and gave out a heavy sigh. He went to start up the car. Jackie panicked.

"Okay, baby, I'll do it. Please don't be mad!"

Taquan looked at her smiling. "That's the way to be, baby." He reached for the lever on the side of the seat and dropped the front seat down. "Take off your panties, baby. I've got something for you."

He leaned over and ran his hand up her inner thigh. When he reached her pussy he sat back with a start. "Where's your panties, bitch?" he snarled.

Jackie thought fast. "I didn't wear any tonight. I thought we were going to the motel and I wanted to surprise you."

Taquan looked at her suspiciously. And then he smiled. "You're hot, baby. I like that." He drew his hand back up her thigh and covered her sexual mound. "And you're all wet already. You're the best!"

Taquan lifted Jackie's skirt and, after freeing his cock, climbed on top of her. She spread her legs and let him enter her. It felt strange to have another cock in there so soon after Leo's.

Taquan was gentle and took his time. He unbuttoned her blouse and freed her breasts. He didn't comment on the lack of a bra. He married his lips to hers and washed her mouth with his tongue. Jackie felt herself begin to get aroused in spite of herself. Soon they were fucking like there was no tomorrow. Jackie reveled in the feel of his iron hard cock and her mind was awash with joy at the knowledge that she had not been found out.

As he drove her home, Jackie got the courage to speak to him about Leo.

"I don't want to go with Leo any more, Taquan," she said timidly.

"What's the matter with Leo?" Taquan responded. "I thought that you liked him."

"I want to be with you, baby," she said. "And no, I don't like him."

Taquan's hands gripped the steering wheel tightly. "He didn't try anything with you, did he?" he asked his voice angry and tense. "I'll fuck him up good!"

Jackie felt fear run through her. She didn't want Taquan going up against Leo. The older man was mean and violent. She didn't want to see Taquan hurt or even killed.

"No, baby!" she protested. "He didn't do anything! It's just the way he looks at me, that's all."

"If he ever touches you, you tell me right away," Taquan responded, sounding relieved yet determined. "I'll know what to do."

"Please, honey," Jackie begged. "He didn't touch me, honest. I just don't want to go with him anymore, that's all."

"Just a couple more times, baby," Taquan said pleadingly. They had pulled up a block from Jackie's house. "I'm almost clear. Please, do it for me."

Jackie felt a lump in her throat as she nodded okay. He gave her a deep, soulful kiss. "See you in a week or so, baby," he said. "Be good."

That night, Jackie took a long, hot bath. She didn't feel like she would ever be clean. Her head pounded from the booze and the coke and she threw up twice. She took out the aspirator from the medicine closet and jetted soapy water up her pussy several times. When she got into bed, she cried herself to sleep.

It was only two days later that she saw Taquan waiting at the street corner on her way home from school. They made a date for that night. But when he picked her up, he drove her to where Leo's car was waiting.

This time, Leo didn't bother with the nightclub. He drove the unhappy girl right to a motel. When they got inside the room, he told her to strip.

Leo sat on the edge of the bed while Jackie knelt naked in front of him and serviced him with her mouth. He had stripped too and she was repelled by his huge, obese body. He had let her do a couple lines before they got started. He fucked her for three hours. Not continuously, but, intermittently, drinking and doing some more coke each time after he dumped a load into her. He made her come too, each time. And he had her lie down on the bed, her legs spread while he tongued her twat for half an hour. She cried and begged him to stop after she came twice, but he wasn't satisfied until she came for the third time, moaning loudly, her whole body shivering and shaking.

Over the next three weeks, she saw Leo four times. Each time, on the way to the motel, she silently bemoaned her upcoming ordeal while shamefully knowing that the fat man would drive her to several mind numbing orgasms and that she would moan and cry out louder than Taquan had ever made her. After each night with Leo, Taquan drove her to their spot and fucked her too. She spent her days sad and depressed. She was falling behind in school and she missed track practice twice. She started looking forward to the coke that Leo was giving her and each time that they went to the motel, she did as many lines as she could until her mind was numb.

Each night, Leo took her panties home with him. He started to give her money when they were done. A fifty one night and a hundred another. "You're worth it baby," he told her. She thought about refusing it, but didn't want to make the man angry. Since she didn't have pockets in her skirt, she had to clench the bill in her hand while Taquan fucked her later.

Then Leo disappeared. She and Taquan went out on dates again. It seemed like things were getting back to the way they were. Her work at school started to improve and she won a couple of races. One night, about a month after the last time she had gone out with Leo, Taquan told her, after he picked her up, that she was going to go out with Leo that night. Jackie's heart felt like lead. She had thought that it was all over.

"One last time," Taquan promised. When they pulled up to where they were going to meet Leo, the fat man wasn't there yet. Taquan pulled Jackie's body to him and kissed her. She felt like crying, but held it in. "One last time," she thought hopefully.

She felt Taquan's hand reach under her skirt. She broke their kiss, startled. "Just checking, baby," he told her. "I've been getting suspicious you coming back without your panties every time you see Leo. If you come back without them tonight, I'll know."

Jackie's heart fell when Leo's black Caddy pulled around the corner. She was in a dilemma. How would she make Leo give her back her panties at the end of the night? Maybe she should refuse to go with him? But Taquan would know then that there was something going on. Maybe if she held on to them after she took them off? She would figure something out. This was the last time and she didn't want to ruin everything now.

Instead of driving to the motel, like Jackie expected, they drove to a tall, fancy apartment building. There was a parking garage under it and Leo pulled into a spot way in the back. "We're going to a party, honey," he told her as he turned off the engine. "But first I want a little taste."

He pulled Jackie towards him with his powerful arm and held her body close to his while he jammed his tongue into her mouth. She tried to struggle, but he was too powerful. She felt the seat fall back and he pushed her down. "Please, not here," she begged as he lay atop her.

"Don't worry, baby, nobody's coming. I'll be quick."

Jackie felt the man's hand reach under her skirt. She tried to grab it, but his monstrous arm just kept going. She felt him tug on her panties and she struggled all the more. But he soon had them down around her knees. She was afraid that he was going to tear them off of her and so she gave up her efforts to preserve them and let him slide them over her feet.

He was right when he said that he was going to be quick. He played with her labia while kissing her mouth until her moisture began to be released. It was still hard going when he entered her and she moaned in discomfort.

But his motions soon caused her juices to flow and his cock began to move in and out of her easily. Her lusts were just starting to rise when he came with a loud groan.

"See baby, I wasn't lyin'," he said as he zipped himself up. Jackie sat up and reached for her panties. He beat her to them.

"You know I need these, baby," he said, grinning. "I've got a whole drawer full now."

"Please, I need them," Jackie said plaintively.

"You don't need them, honey. You'll make me all hot thinking about your bare pussy all night."

"No," Jackie said insistently. "I really need them."

Leo held them up, twirling them around his fat fingers. "What for?" he asked.

"He'll know if I don't have them later," she said, her eyes tearing. "He knows I was wearing panties tonight. He'll check when I get back."

"Taquan?" Leo asked laughing. "How will he know?" Jackie just looked at the callous man dolefully.

"You mean you've been fucking him every night after I drop you off?" Leo asked, disbelief in his voice. He laughed heartily. "Don't I give you enough, baby? I'll have to do better."

Jackie was mortified that Leo now knew that she made love to Taquan every night after he was done with her. She felt like such a slut. But that was what she had become. Leo had made her one. But she didn't want to lose Taquan. She would do anything to prevent him from finding out what she had been doing with Leo all of these weeks.

"Please," Jackie asked again, whining. "I'll be good to you tonight, I promise."

Leo laughed again. "You're a real hot bitch, lady!" he exclaimed. "A natural born whore. You just can't get enough dick to keep you happy."

"It's not like that," Jackie protested. But the words turned to dust in her mouth. If it wasn't like that, what was it like?

"I tell you what, bitch," Leo said. "If you're real good to me tonight and do whatever I say, I'll give them back to you. Okay?"

Jackie quailed at what the terrible man could mean by 'whatever he said'. But she had no choice. "Okay," she sad unhappily.

The apartment they were going to was on the 21st floor and Jackie's stomach turned over as the elevator came to a stop. Leo knocked on the door of apartment 2112. There was the faint noise of a party escaping from behind the door, a sound that increased in volume when the door opened. A pretty black woman answered. She had her black hair done up in a bouffant and she was wearing a clinging, tight yellow shift that ended about six inches above her knees. She looked to be in her middle thirties. There was a slit up the side going almost all the way to her hip.

"Leo, baby!" she shouted. She jumped forwards and gave him a big hug. And then she looked at Jackie. "Ooooooo! She's hot!" she said. "Where you been hiding this young thing?"

"Meet Jackie, Luanda. She's come to party hardy," he said laughing.

"Well, then, come on in!"

Leo seemed to know everybody. There were five black men of varying ages sitting around a table playing poker and two other men sitting on a couch with pretty, barely dressed girls on their laps. Jackie was told all of their names, but she didn't really catch any of them. Leo took her into the kitchen where he laid out two long, thick lines of coke. "Come on, honey," he told the young, uncomfortable girl, "get started."

She didn't like the fact that she was at a party with no panties on. But getting a little tooted would help her relax. She did a line quickly.

"Do the other one too, baby," Leo told her. "We've got some catching up to do."

Obediently, Jackie leaned over the table to do the other line. She wanted to get blasted. It was the only way that she could deal with her nervousness. She just had to get her panties back.

As she drew the line of white powder up her nose, she felt Leo's hand reach under her skirt and caress her bare ass. She stood up with a jerk. "What are you doing?" she asked indignantly. The man had her panties in his other hand and was twirling them around.

"Whatever I want, baby. Whatever I want," he answered.

Someone made them some drinks and Leo sat down at the poker table. He pulled out a fat cigar and made Jackie sit behind him and to his left. She watched the game morosely as she drank her drink. When she finished it, one of the girls got her another one. After about a half hour, Leo took her back into the kitchen where she did a couple more lines. This time, as he caressed her naked buttocks, she let him.

"This is a fucking stupid party," Jackie thought as she sat watching the card game. There was loud music coming from a CD player, but that was the only 'party' thing about it. She did notice that the women kept on going back and forth into the bedrooms with the men, a different one each time. They would leave and, later, there would be a knock on the door and more would come in. Before they went in the bedrooms, the men would hand the women money which they would put into a slot in the lid of a big can on the counter.

Jackie was sitting in her chair dazed and bored when Leo told her to get up and come closer to him. He had just pulled in a large pile of cash. "You're my good luck charm, baby," he said as he wrapped his arm around her hip. Jackie was uncomfortable about him touching her in front of all these older people and she tried to pull away. Leo just held her tighter.

"What's the matter, Jackie? Don't you like your big daddy? Give me a kiss."

The big man took her arm and pulled her onto his lap. Circling his other hand around her head, he forced her lips to his. Jackie whined and struggled, but finally let his tongue into her mouth. He was holding her tightly and she was unable to stop him from running his hand up her thigh and under her skirt. She gave a muffled, "Noooooo!", but he soon had her thigh all the way to her hip exposed.

"Whoooooeeeee!" one of the men said. "That's hot stuff!" The other men laughed and agreed.

Leo broke their kiss and announced to the small crowd, "Jackie goes commando! Don't you honey? You like to show off your pretty pussy, don't you?"

Jackie squirmed free of Leo's lap, but he took hold of her arm and forced her to stand next to him. "Why don't you show the boys your pretty pussy, Jackie? Lift your skirt up so they can see."

Leo's question was met by hoots and hollers. Jackie blushed, mortified at what Leo was suggesting. "No!" she shouted emphatically as she struggled to free her arm from Leo's grasp. "Let me go! I want to go home!"

Leo merely pulled her panties from his sports jacket pocket. He twirled them around on his hand like he had done in the kitchen. "You promised to be nice to me baby," he reminded her. "Whatever I said, remember?"

"What you got there, Leo?" one of the men called out.

"These are Jackie's panties, Leroy," Leo answered. "I took them from her when I fucked her downstairs in my car before we came up. If she don't get them back, her boyfriend's going to be real mad."

The men all laughed. "Who's her boyfriend?" one of the men asked.

"Ya all know Taquan, don't you?" Leo asked, still twirling the panties. Jackie could not keep her eyes off of them. She was shamed and embarrassed that Leo had told the people that they had fucked in his car. She was starting to get a bad feeling about how things were going to turn out tonight.

"Taquan?" the man replied. "That bad boy? He'll fuck her up good if he finds out."

"Yeah, me and Jackie been going at it for weeks now right under his very nose. I wouldn't want to be her when he finds out. He checked her panties tonight before she went out and if she comes back without them, well, I wouldn't want to be her."

Jackie thought about Leo's statement. Would Taquan hurt her? It was inconceivable, after all, that he would go after Leo. She would be the most likely target of his anger.

And then he would leave her. She felt like she was going to cry.

"Come on honey," Leroy said. "Show us your pussy. Do what the man say."

Jackie didn't know what to do. She feared that showing the men her sex would lead to other, unhappy things. But Leo had her panties. She just couldn't go home without them. She stood there, immobilized.

"Luanda," Leo called out, "get me a pair of scissors."

Jackie turned to him in dismay. "Pleeeeease," she whined.

The tall, good looking whore went into the kitchen and returned with a pair of scissors with a bright orange handle. Smiling, she handed them to Leo.

"Now, honey, you don't have to do anything," he said to Jackie. "You can go on home right now. No one's going to stop you. But these panties are going to be in little pieces in about ten seconds if you don't do what I told you. These folks are my friends and if you're going to embarrass me in front of them, then you're just going to have to pay the consequences." He opened the scissors and put her delicate, bright yellow bikini panties between them. "If you want," he said, "I'll count to three."

A chill ran through Jackie as she saw her panties in peril. Her eyes were wet with tears. "Please, don't," she whined unhappily. "I'll do it."

Jackie reached her hands down to the hem of her short skirt and raised it slowly up. Everyone's attention was on her coffee colored thighs as it came higher and higher. When it rose above her bushy, brown, pubic hair, there was an outburst of merriment.

"Hot damn," Leroy shouted. "That's one fine pussy you got there girl!" The other men were in agreement. Jackie held her skirt up around her waist for a few moments and then it drop.

"No, no, no!" Leo barked. "Keep it up. Let everybody get a good look!"

Jackie obediently lifted it again. Leo made her walk around the table so that all the men could get a better view of her moss covered pussy. They all made appreciative exclamations and joked. One of the men pulled her body close to him and started running his powerful hand over her mound. She struggled and cried until he finally let her go. When she returned to where Leo sat, he pulled her up on his lap.

"That's a good girl," he said. "Now you sit right here and bring me some luck.

Jackie sat unhappily on the big man's legs for the next few hands. Before tonight, there had been only two men who had ever seen her pussy, Taquan and Leo. And now all these strange men had. She felt dirty and ashamed.

Leo poured a few shots of bourbon for her and had her do a couple more lines of coke. His hands were all over her and she squirmed and protested meekly as his fingers stroked her pussy or his hand pressed on and massaged her breasts. Every once in a while, he would pull her lips to his and slip his tongue into her mouth. She tried to fight him off by pushing at his massive chest, but he was strong and she was too weak. Her head was getting woozier and woozier and the contact of Leo's hot hand with her naked skin, his fondling of her breasts and the sensation of his tongue swirling around in her mouth was starting to arouse her.

He had another idea. "Hey," he said to the men at the table. "Who wants to see Jackie's tits?"

The men gave a general, enthusiastic assent. "Okay," Leo said, "my pile's getting a little small. Why don't you guys all chip in ten bucks each and I show you Jackie's titties? I can tell you that they're worth it."

The men happily tossed tens and fives across the table to Leo. When he had collected them, he started to unbutton Jackie's blouse. She had been startled when he made the proposition to the men but too stoned to react. When she felt Leo's hand on the top button, she raised her hands and tried to push his strong, black hands away. "Noooooo," she whined softly. Leo merely grabbed her arms and brought them behind her back. He circled his right arm around them and held them close to his body, trapping them in place. "Come on, baby," he said in a mock, pleading voice. "Everybody wants to see what you've got, and they've already paid. I can't just give them their money back. That wouldn't be right. You don't want your money back boys, do you?"

The other men, laughing, certified Leo's assessment of their desires. With a practiced hand, Leo began to undo the buttons of Jackie's pretty, white blouse. It had a deep 'v' neck so as to show off the pleasant, plump tops of her mounds and so as soon as the first button was released, her delicate, lacey bra was revealed. Jackie cried as Leo unfastened one button after another until her blouse swung free.

There were appropriate oohs and ahhs as Jackie's lacy underthing was exposed. Her large breasts filled the small, half cups attractively. They swayed as she struggled in Leo's firm grasp. The pretty garment had a clasp in the front and Leo deftly flicked it open with his one hand.

Jackie's full, milk chocolate colored mounds burst free from their enclosures. She had fat, short nipples and a two inch wide, silky smooth areola around each one. The girl moaned and squirmed on Leo's lap unhappily. She could see that the men's lusts were being enflamed by the exposure of her treasures. She was afraid of what they would do to her. Her pretty, little, yellow panties were on the table, next to Leo's pile of cash. If she could only get them she would run out the door. She still had her clothes on, even though her blouse and bra were unbuttoned, but she could deal with that. She could walk or call someone to come get her, a girlfriend or something, if she could get to a phone.

But Jackie's scheming was rudely interrupted when Leo reached his hands to the neck of her blouse and quickly pulled it over her shoulders, carrying the straps to her dainty bra with it. Jackie was frightened and woozy from the coke and booze and her reactions, normally swift and sure, were delayed. By the time she knew it, Leo had her upper coverings down past her elbows and was slipping them over her hands.

"Ohhhhh!" she cried out. She tried to cover her breasts with her hands, but Leo grabbed them and brought them back behind her. He held her waist tightly with one strong arm and pulled her against his body, trapping her arms.

"What did I tell you, fellas," Leo stated proudly. "They're quite a set, ain't they?" He received no disagreement. He took one of her breasts in his meaty hand and gave it a gentle squeeze so that the nipple stood put prominently. Jackie whined and struggled on his lap. She looked around the table at the five, rough looking, older, black men and she saw no faces likely to come to her aid. The women who had been whoring all night were standing around the table watching. Although they were dressed scantily, attired in colorful, lacy teddies, they were not naked as she practically was. She saw no sympathy there, either, only the looks of women who had seen this kind of thing happen before, who probably experienced a similar initiation into their profession years ago. And they had undoubtedly learned the hard way not to interfere with Leo when he was on the game.

Leo continued to massage and play with Jackie's naked breasts while the poker game resumed. He fed Jackie a couple more shots of bourbon. She refused, at first, but a little tweak to one of her exposed nipples convinced her to open her mouth and down the hot, rough liquor. While the other men dealt the cards, called the play, made their bets, Leo stroked Jackie's soft, naked skin. He ran his hands over her thighs and under her skirt. She tried to close her legs, muttering "Don't, please," but Leo intertwined his strong legs with hers and pulled her knees apart. His hand took possession of the soft mound between her thighs, raising her skirt so that her pussy was exposed, and continued the explorations that he had begun earlier. As the tantalizing sensations of his expert strokes ran through her, Jackie felt her lusts begin to rise. She struggled to free her hands, but Leo just held her all the more tightly. She closed her eyes to try and make the exciting sensations go away, but they continued as her captor rubbed firmly, but gently, in practiced round strokes, her bud of pleasure. She could feel the eyes of the gamblers on her, even with her shut eyes, and she was ashamed to be made into a display for their prurient enjoyment. When Leo leaned over and captured a nipple between his fat lips, sucking hard while his tongue teased it, Jackie gave out a moan of surrender.

The unhappy girl's body ceased her combat against Leo's manipulation of her sex and she let her legs relax their strain against their imprisonment. The moan attracted the attention of the men at the card table and they called out encouragement to both her and Leo.

"Go, man!" she heard the fellow called Leroy shout out. Another man said, "Come on baby, let it all out! Come on! Come on!"

Leo responded gleefully to his friends' enthusiasm. "Ya'll want to see her come?" he asked, his hand deep in her pussy. They responded in unison their enthusiastic assent. "Ya'll want to se her come?" Leo asked again tauntingly.

He increased his agitation of Jackie's quim. As her lust grew higher and higher, Jackie leaned her head back on his immense shoulder. At his proffer to the men, her befogged mind tried to take a last stand. She squirmed and made another effort to free her hands behind her. "Noooooo," she said softly, "pleeeeeease." She could feel the tingling of her pussy that denoted its impending explosion even as her mind rebelled against it. She bit her lip to suppress her cries of ecstasy. Leo called out one more time, "Ya'll want to see her come?"

This time the men were vociferous in their response. Leo slid two thick fingers inside Jackie's feverish canal. He continued to stroke her hardened, electrified clit with his thumb. "Pleeeeeeeeease stop! Please!" Jackie called out frantically just before her passions crested. "Ahhhhhh! Ahhhhhhhh! Ahhhhhhhhhhh!" she shouted as her crevasse exploded with pleasure. Her pussy clamped around her assailant's fat fingers which continued to saw back and forth within her. Her body shuddered and her large, pleasing, mammaries bounced and swayed. She raised her hips to meet the digit that was tormenting her energized pleasure nubbin. "Ahhhhhhh!" she called out at each intense, pleasure giving contraction of her loins. "Ahhhhhhh! Ahhhhhhhhh!"

As her tremors of delight ebbed, a wave of shame and misery passed though the poor girl. What the men had seen was something that she had not wanted them to. It was bad enough that she had succumbed to pleasure at Leo's hands while at his mercy at the motel or in his car. But now she had proven herself a lustful whore, displayed and teased to pleasure for the amusement of unknown men.

Tears flowed down the unhappy girl's face as Leo continued to manhandle her, rubbing her breasts and thighs. "She's somthin', ain't she?" he asked the men. He picked up her panties from the table and took a swipe of her discharge from her flowered, flowing gash and passed it around so that the men could sniff it. Finally, Jackie heard from one of the men what she had been afraid that she would hear ever since Leo made her show them her pussy.

"How much to fuck her?" the man called Leroy asked. Two other men repeated the question.

"Welllllll," Leo drawled, seeming to consider the point. "It will be her first time on the game, and that should count for something. She's got a sweet, tight pussy, I can vouch for that. But I don't want to be greedy. Let's say this. Play out a hand of seven card stud. Whoever wins gets to fuck Jackie and will split the pot with me. Deal?"

There was general assent all around. Jackie tried to get up from Leo's lap as the initial cards were dealt, but he held her firmly in place. She tried to beg him to let her go, not to make her fuck any of the other men. "Oh, please don't do this, please," she whined. Finally, Leo got so sick of it that he picked up her panties and jammed them into her mouth. She moaned and coughed as he shoved them in, filling her oral space and spreading her wide, enticing lips.

The forcibly silenced girl watched miserably, her hands still trapped behind her, as the game progressed. Leo kept her on the boil by continuing to stroke her soft, fur covered pussy and suck at her teats. The men all joked and kept staring at her, their desire for her clear on their faces. When the seventh card was dealt down and dirty, two men were left in. One was Leroy, the most vociferous of her admirers. The other was a taciturn, muscular, broad shouldered man in his late thirties and with a shiny bald head. He was wearing a white sleeveless t-shirt and had a thick, gold chain around his neck. His clean shaven face was jet black and slick with sweat. Jackie noticed that he had tattoos up and down his bulging arms, strange, geometric symbols. His hands were large and carried marks as well, letters, numbers and crosses crudely tattooed across his fingers. Jackie had seen tattoos like that before. Her uncle Jed had been in prison years ago and he wore similar markings. Unhappily resigned to being fucked by one of the men, she hoped that it wasn't him, but the more easy going and less cruel looking Leroy.

But when Leroy was called by the black skinned man, Leroy's full house, queens over threes, gave way to the other man's kings over twos. The big man gave out a large grin and hauled the money in. When he counted it out, it was more than six hundred dollars. Smiling, he tossed a wad of cash over to Leo who was sitting across the table from him.

Jackie wailed as the man rose from his seat to claim her. Leo gave her a little shove off of his lap. The distraught girl tried to push the big man away, but he grabbed her hair at the top of her head and pulled at it until she gave out an anguished cry. "Be still, bitch!" he yelled at her. Jackie stopped her caterwauling, reducing them to moans, but she grabbed the hand that was tormenting her scalp with both of hers, futilely trying to free her hair.

"Don't wear her out, Roderick," Leo told the winner of Jackie's flesh. "You've got a half an hour."

"Shiiiiit!" Roderick spat back. "You got over three hundred bucks there. That makes this the most expensive pussy I ever bought. What I'm going to do to this ho 'll take at least an hour."

Roderick was clearly not the type to be intimidated. Leo laughed. "Okay, okay," he said. "Just don't mark her all up. And leave some for the rest of the boys," he added.

As the man pulled Jackie towards the bedrooms, she began to fight and claw at him. She tried to scream her refusal, but her gagged mouth let out only muffled wails. "…oooooooh! …oooooooooh!" she cried as the giant, muscular hand propelled her to her doom. By the time they got to the bedroom doorway, Jackie was being dragged across the floor. Her naked breasts were swaying and jerking and the coarse rug burned her hip and her knees as she was, nonetheless, moved quickly and efficiently into the room.

The bedroom was simply decorated. A cheap, pressed wood dresser stained like dark oak, a small bedside table with a lamp on it. The bed was a double bed and had a large, battered headboard. There were no blankets, only a sheet and two worn out, lumpy pillows. The bedside lamp was the only light in the room and, after the well lit living room where Jackie had spent most of the evening, the dim light seemed ominous.

Jackie's head was swirling with the booze and dope but she had a heightened awareness of what was going on. She was about to be raped. And although outside the small bedroom was a room full of people, some of them women, she knew that no one would help her. She tried to scream out from her gagged mouth, but the sound barely made an echo on the bare walls of the room.

When Roderick tossed her body on the bed, Jackie tried to get up and run from the room. He grabbed her hand and gave her a fierce slap across the face, stunning her. "Cut the shit, bitch!" he yelled. He pulled her to the mattress, face down and put his heavy weight on top of her. Jackie tried to rise, but there was no way. She heard the man loosening the belt to his pants and then heard the tell tale sound of it being swished through his pant's loops.

In a second or two, the man had circled Jackie's flailing wrists with the belt and tied them together. He dragged her hands to the head of the bed and fastened it there. He got off of her and ably flipped her to her back.

Jackie face still burned where she had been slapped and she moaned with fear as the jet black face of the man looked down at her exposed and vulnerable breasts. "You sure have nice tits, honey," he told her. He played with them briefly, tugging at her stiffened nipples, mashing them against her chest. He then looked her directly in the eyes. "Now," he said to her in an evil, deep voice full of hatred and cruelty, "if you give me any more trouble, I'm going to hurt you real bad. I don't care what Leo says. He may think that he's badass, but he don't know what badass is. I'm badass and you better believe it!"

The bound and half naked eighteen year old girl had never been so frightened in her life. There was a level of harshness to this man that surpassed anything she had ever experienced. She nodded her tear stained face dolefully.

Roderick smiled and got up from the bed. Jackie watched, mesmerized as he stripped off his black, baggy denims and his t-shirt. His chest muscles rippled, the result, Jackie surmised, of years of weight lifting in the exercise yard at Joliet or some other prison down state. He was wearing a pair of dark red sport jockeys and his loins were packed tight in a big, ominous lump beneath them. When he tore them off and threw them to the floor, Jackie saw his long, thick, tumescent manhood and she moaned with unhappiness.

Roderick climbed on the bed and threw his large, muscular leg over Jackie's bare tummy. He sat there for a while, his stiffening cock lying on her belly, while he played some more with her ample breasts. Jackie moaned and cried, hating the feel of his strong, relentless hands on her tender mounds, squealing with pain when he squeezed them harshly. She pulled and twisted her hands in a vain attempt to free them, but it seemed like the man had done this before, since she was unable to gain any slack in the leather knot that held her wrists joined above her.

The big, solid and finely sculpted, black skinned man moved his body up Jackie's prone torso until his knees were on the sides of her uplifted arms. Jackie knew what he was going to do and moaned with unhappiness. He pulled her pretty panties from her mouth and tossed them aside. "I don't want no teeth," he told her callously. "Just tongue and mouth, you got that?"

Jackie nodded her head in dismal agreement. He placed his large hand on her face and squeezed her cheeks, forcing her mouth into a little 'o', and presented the head of his thick, hardened cock to it. Jackie's stomach did a turn as he slid it over her tongue and into her mouth.

Roderick took his time in plowing Jackie's mouth. He pushed himself all the way to the edge of her throat and then back again slowly and with deliberation. His hard belly pressed against her forehead and his large, soft balls rested on her chin. She cried and gagged when he pushed into her throat, twisting and turning her hips and legs as she fought for air and to keep the bile that rose from her belly from spilling out. He kept murmuring a repeated series of "Oh, yeahs!" as he coursed his cock along her tongue and lips. She kept her lips formed into a little 'o' to make sure that her teeth made no contact with his thick, soft textured shaft as it ran up and down in her defenseless, tormented mouth. She had heard of what her girlfriends had called 'face fucking' and realized that that was what the man was doing to her. Her powerlessness to oppose him and the callous way that he was using her made her mind swoon with humiliation and shame. The thick meat scoured her mouth again and again, a brutal, offensive intruder that became the focus of her entire body and mind. Tears flowed from her eyes in torrents and she tried hard to withhold her sobs, fearing that the man would get mad and hurt her. Each time that his fat cock struck the back of her mouth, she made a piteous, involuntary, "gaaaaa!" sound and a wave of nausea swept through her.

Jackie had begun to think that her torment would go on forever. She was shamed and humiliated but, at the same time relieved, when she felt the cock begin to pulse and jerk within her mouth. She coughed and sputtered as she tried to swallow his warm, gooey discharge, but the volume of his release and the repeated forceful and rapid jamming of his cock into her mouth caused some of it to spill out over her lips and down her cheeks and chin.

Roderick signaled the end of his ejaculations with a long, deep, "Ahhhhhhhh!" He pulled his softening cock from her lips and eased off of her. "That was great, baby," he told her. "You're a natural."

Jackie happily thought that he had forgotten his pledge to fuck her for a whole hour when he left the room for a minute. When he left, she desperately tried to free her bound hands. But he had just gone to get a bottle of Hiram Walker and a glass. Her heart sunk when she saw the door opening again. He poured himself a large shot and downed it in one gulp. Then he poured another and he proffered it to Jackie's lips.

Since the man had returned, the girl had been laying there on her side, her knees all scrunched up to her belly, bemoaning her fate. This was all because she had agreed to do Taquan a favor and had not the courage to tell him that Leo had assaulted her. What a fool she was, she thought. She felt fouled and dirtied, both by Leo's lascivious manhandling of her in front of the men and her shameful reaction, and because she had let the man fuck her throat. She knew that she had no ability to stop him, but something inside her told her that she should have resisted more, refused to cooperate no matter what he did to her.

The fact that she didn't, to her twisted logic, made her indeed what the men had called her, a whore.

Despondent that her torment was not yet done, anxious to blot from her mind her responsibility for what had happened to her, she accepted the whisky readily. She coughed and moaned as it went down. She watched as Roderick picked her wet and balled up panties from the floor. When he presented them to her lips, she broke out anew into tears and asked him piteously, "Please, please don't." He paid her no mind and jammed them between her teeth.

Roderick lay himself down next to her on the bed and began to run his hands all over her body. She was still wearing her stylish, yellow high heels, picked out to match the flouncy, yellow and black checkered miniskirt that she still wore around her hips. Roderick pulled it up around her waist so that the fabric was bunched together like a little belt, exposing all below it.

At first, her skin crawled as she felt his surprisingly soft and gentle touch range over her belly and thighs, over her breasts and shoulders, her hips and her sex. When he began to kiss her thick, prominent nipples, she sighed unwillingly. When his hand reached between her thighs and captured her pussy, stroking one long, thick finger the length of the slit between her engorged outer lips, she moaned. He turned his body towards her feet and she felt his strong hands on the insides of her thighs, pushing them apart.

Jackie groaned with unwanted pleasure as his lips found her little bud. It was rigid with attentiveness from his caresses and he sucked on it soothingly and gently as he ran his tongue back and forth over it slowly. She made a weak effort to bring her thighs together, but the man's hands held them firmly apart. She moaned and twisted her body as he tormented her enflamed slit, running his hot tongue down it again and again. His hands caressed her inner thighs softly, making them shudder. She felt her juices rising and she gave one last feeble effort to push his ardent tongue away by thrusting up on her hips and kicking her feet.

Jackie screamed into her stuffed mouth when she came. Her shoes pounded on the mattress and she pulled and yanked on the bindings that held her wrists. Roderick didn't stop after her first orgasm, but kept her going until she was on the verge of boiling over yet again. Sensing that she was near, he turned his body and climbed between her thighs. When he entered her, she gave out a loud, groan and her pussy went into convulsions. He continued to give her pussy languid, determined strokes of his thick meat until she came again and then he spilled himself inside her.

Roderick drank some more while he waited for his forces to rise again and made her swallow more of it too. After he fucked her from behind, her hips raised and her breasts scraping the coarse sheet of the bed, he left. He patted her on the ass and told her enthusiastically that he would see her again, "real soon!" He left his belt behind.

Another man came in when he left and then another. They used her mouth and her pussy brutally. After the fourth man, two of the whores came in and took her to the bathroom and cleaned her off, letting her pee. They had to support her wobbling form as she could hardly stand from the sex, booze and drugs. They returned her to the bedroom and, after straightening out her skirt, sat her back down on the bed. Leo came in as soon as the women left and gave her two more lines to do. Unbeknownst to her, he had laced the coke with a little meth so that she wouldn't pass out. He fucked her himself then, waiting to discharge until she shuddered through another tormented orgasm and, when he was finished, retied her hands to the wood at the head of the bed.

The room was full of light when Jackie awoke the next morning. Her head was pounding and her body felt like it had been pummeled by a hundred fists. She did not remember how many men had fucked her, but they had kept coming all night. The insides of her thighs were bruised from an unknown number of callous, lustful hips slamming against them. Her jaw was aching from the all cocks that she had sucked. Her pretty miniskirt, which they had left on her all night as a kind of decoration, was smeared with dried cum and the leakage from her well used pussy. She moaned with misery when she saw that it was day. From the strength of the light coming in the room, she realized that it was late in the morning. Her hands had been untied from the headboard at some point and she wrapped them around her body in misery.

Luanda came in shortly afterwards. She made Jackie get up and took her into the shower where, after stripping herself, she stepped in and washed her. She sat the miserable, defeated girl on the toilet and brushed out her long, black hair. She didn't say anything to Jackie. It was understood that what had happened to her the night before was horrible and insufferable, but also that there was nothing that the older whore was going to do about it. Leo was in the kitchen eating a huge sandwich when Jackie emerged from the bathroom, having been permitted to restore her skirt and blouse. He motioned for her to sit on the couch in the living room and wait for him.

The fat whoremaster drove her home. To her chagrin he dropped her off in front of her house. As she went to get out, he handed her her panties.

Jackie's mother and father were beside themselves. They saw her emerge from the big, black Cadillac, saw the shady fat man that was driving it. But no matter how many "where you been all night!" they shouted at her, or how many times her father slapped her, she said nothing about her shameful ordeal. It was too late to go to school and so Jackie slept the rest of the day and into the evening. She emerged only to drink a glass of water and then returned to bed.

Jackie's mother and father insisted that she go to school the next day. Jackie sat through her classes morose and silent. Usually an active participant in the day's discussions, she just stared at her open book, seeing nothing. Her biology teacher sent her to the nurse, but Jackie merely told the old, grey haired black woman that she was tired and had her, 'friend'. The kindly woman let her lay down in the nurse's office for the rest of the day, a comforting, warm heating pad on her tummy.

Three days later, on her way home from school, Jackie saw Leo's car parked next to the curb. She had still not shaken off her depression about what had been done to her. Her parents had been treating her as a pariah. Jackie saw the passenger side door of Leo's Caddy open and out stepped Taquan. He was smiling and called her name. Meekly, not knowing what else to do, she got into the car at his invitation, sliding along the long, bench seat in the front until her hip touched up to the grinning Leo's. "Hiya, baby," he said.

Taquan got in next to her and slammed the door shut. When they got a few blocks away from where they had picked her up, Taquan took her books and school bag from her. He looked at them briefly and then, lowering the electric window, tossed them out into the street.

And so Jackie became one of Leo's whores. Both he and Taquan fucked her when they got back to the apartment, making her service them with her mouth first. And that night she went to work. The other girls were sweet and nice to her, mostly, but Leo and Taquan were mean and cruel. Roderick came back a couple of times as promised and she groaned and screamed with pleasure when he fucked her. But most of the other men produced nothing but little moans from her. She learned, though, to demonstrate more enthusiasm after one night when, her hands tied to the headboard of the bed and her legs spread and tied off to the posts at its foot, Leo whipped her cruelly with his belt for half an hour. He had placed some duct tape over her mouth to stifle her screams. After that, whether the men produced sexual excitement for her or not, she made them think that they did.

Taquan used her mostly as a convenience, fucking her or getting her to suck him off when he stopped by. He worked for Leo, of course, and he managed the street girls for him. Luanda told her repeatedly that she had better do a good job with the johns or she would end up there herself, cruising the Loop at all kinds of hours and in all kinds of weather, fucking or sucking off twenty or thirty men a day.

On the other hand, Leo, when he had the time and inclination, would fuck her for hours, making her come again and again, screaming with delight. He was good at what he did and all the girls liked to fuck him.

Once, a couple weeks after she became a full fledged whore, some white detectives came around asking about her. It seemed that her parents had filed a missing persons report. Leo knew them both and laughed and shared drinks with them as Jackie sucked them off. He handed them a small wad of cash when they left.

From time to time, Leo had Taquan take Jackie to a fancy hotel for an assignation. She would get all dressed up and Luanda would help her with her makeup. It was the only times that she left the five bedroom apartment and the only time that she got fully dressed. All the other times she walked around the apartment, like the other girls, nude or dressed in a lacy chemise and panties or a short, revealing teddy.

It was on one of these assignations that Jackie made her break. She had been with Leo about a year and a half. She spent most of her time in a haze. She drank whatever booze was proffered to her and she eagerly snorted up Leo's coke or stuff belonging to a john whenever she could. The group had become her new, dysfunctional, but ever present family, replacing the one that had all but disappeared after her brother, Johnny was killed. She had seen some of the girls come and go and she had begun to realize that a dismal future awaited her. Twice, new girls had been brought in and older girls sent to work the streets with Taquan.

The john with who she had a date was an older white man. He was obviously rich from his clothes and his mannerisms. He fell asleep after she sucked him off. He had left his wallet on the bedside table and it had about seven hundred dollars in it. Determined to escape, Jackie took the money and went down the back elevator of the hotel. She didn't know what to do or where to go. She was dressed in a flashy, red dress that came up to within a few inches of her pussy. Her breasts spilled out of the scanty bodice and she was wearing six inch high heels. Her face was painted like, well, like a whore's.

The only thing Jackie could think of doing was to take a bus out of town. It didn't matter where, just any bus. She hailed a cab and it dropped her off at the Greyhound station. The next bus was to Portland, Oregon, and although she had never been there and had no idea what the place was like, she bought a ticket.

Jackie was sitting on a bench waiting for the bus to leave when Taquan walked in. She had never seen him so mad. He was with two other big guys, men who worked for Leo and sometimes came by for freebees. Jackie gave a squeal and started for the exit on the other side of the terminal. She was struggling in her high heels and so she kicked them off. She knew that even though she hadn't run in almost two years, she could certainly outrun Taquan and his two bullies. She dashed out the glass doors to the street looking behind her to make sure that she was getting distance on the men. When she stepped out onto the sidewalk, she ran right into the arms of Leo.

Leo didn't say anything to her. He simply dragged her over to the car and threw her into the open trunk. He slammed it shut and drove off after the other men got in.

They didn't go back to the apartment. When they let her out of the trunk, she was in what looked like an old factory building. Taquan and one of the other men dragged her down into the basement. Jackie wailed and cried and begged for forgiveness as Leo's boys tore her clothes from her. One of them had a rope and, once she was naked, they bound her hands together in front of her and tossed the free end over a beam. They pulled it taut until Jackie's toes lifted off of the dirty floor.

Leo approached her holding a long, leather whip. He didn't say anything. Jackie's frantic pleas for mercy echoed off of the dirty, stone walls. When the lash first tore into her body, Jackie screamed with pain. It was as if a knife had been dragged across her body. The blow landed across her tight, graceful thighs and left a long red line. The second blow was across her breasts and she screamed with dismay at the fiery leavings. Again and again he whipped her. She struggled at her bonds, causing her body to sway and jerk as the lash bit into her repeatedly. The other men stood around and watched her agony, smoking cigarettes and drinking from a flask. Leo worked up and down her front, decorating her pretty breasts, belly and thighs with a mass of angry red lines. He then shifted to her back and stopped only when he had run out of room to create new marks.

When the whipping finally stopped, Jackie's voice was hoarse from screaming. Her face, the only part of her body unmarred besides her moneymaking pussy, was awash with tears. The leavings of the whip burned her dangling body all over. Her mind was numb with hopelessness.

Leo made her suck him off when they finally let her down. She did so sorrowfully, but energetically, hoping to get back in his good graces. But when he emptied his cock down her throat, he left her there for the other men. Taquan used her brutally and then so did the others. She had no idea how long they kept her in the dirty basement. When they were not abusing her, they kept her tied up in a small closet, wrists to ankles, and a black hood over her head. Sometimes, she felt like they had left there all alone and she cried and tried to yell to see if anyone was there, her voice muffled by the heinous hood, the sounds echoing off the cruel walls of her small prison. She grew afraid that they had had enough of her and had left her to die. Sooner or later, however, she heard sounds outside her tiny room and the door would open and someone would drag her out to fuck her.

There was a dirty, old mattress out in the main area where they abused her, but the floor of the closet was bare, cold, rough concrete. From time to time, they washed her off with cold water from a hose. They made her eat from a bowl on the floor just like a dog and slapped and punched her when she, at first, refused. They kept a five gallon bucket there that she was allowed to piss and shit in.

Jackie's lacerations had faded into thin, barely discernable, white lines when she saw Leo again for the first time since he had whipped her. He was dressed, as usual in a sharp suit and his favorite red ribboned hat, shiny, pointed black shoes. He let her suck his cock and she serviced him with all of the effort and sensuality she could muster. Afterwards, he gave her a thin, cotton robe to put on. She followed him obediently up the stairs from the basement that had been her prison for what seemed like days and days and days and then got into his car.

Life returned to normal at the apartment right away. Some of the johns had missed her and she thanked them politely for their inquiries as to her health. Leo had said that she had been sick and they needed no other explanation than that. The trips to the hotels started up again after a little while, but now Taquan or one of Leo's other men waited outside the hotel room door until she was finished.

But Jackie had not given up all thoughts of escape. While on her outside she was a dutifully merry whore, teasing and cajoling the men out of their money, fucking them like they were sexually omnipotent Adonis's, inside she was desperate and beyond miserable. She got her chance early one morning when Taquan had fallen asleep in her bed. The door to the apartment was usually sealed shut with a large padlock that only he and Leo had the key to. All of the johns had left. Taquan had gotten really loaded that night and, after she had nursed his prick to orgasm twice with her soft sheath, his eyes rolled back and he went to sleep. Jackie tip toed to his pants and pulled out a small, brass key and a few hundred dollars. She had no clothes except for her teddy, but she put it on and found a robe in the bathroom. She threw it over herself and crept quietly but nervously to the door. Her hand shook as she tried to insert the key. She dropped it twice before getting the small implement to slide into the lock. It made a loud 'click' as she turned it open, startling her, and she stopped for a moment to make sure that no one had awakened. When no one responded, she opened the door and stepped out.

The desperate girl was overcome with hysteria as she fled down the stairwell. She did not want to take the elevator for fear of meeting one of Leo's men on the way up. It was cold and rainy outside when she emerged and she realized that she had forgotten shoes. Too frightened to go back, she dashed away into the night.

She was sitting on a bench near the bus station when Jake first saw her. She was too scared to go inside. She was leaning over and sobbing, knowing that it was only a matter of time before she was caught again. She knew that what she suffered last time was only a prelude to what Leo would do to her for a repeat offense. He couldn't have girls running away. It was bad for business. The other girls might get ideas.

Jake was on his way back from a late night jam session with the jazz group that he fooled around with as a sideline. He had decided to walk to get his head clear of the smoke and the gin he had drunk that night, more than usual. He carried his tenor sax in a small case in his left hand. Normally, the sight of a damsel in distress would not have fazed him. But he had just finished a difficult job that had resulted in a twinge to his conscience. And the girl was particularly alluring because of her scanty dress and her naked feet.

Jackie jumped with fear when Jake sat down next to her. At first, she wouldn't say what was the matter and tried to walk away. But Jake grabbed her arm and made her stay. Slowly, but surely, her story came out, at least as much as she could tell him within a few minutes. In an attempt to build up some good karma, Jake invited the girl to come home with him.

Jake lived in an uptown hotel. He didn't have many belongings and he needed a place where he could come and go when he wanted. He fed Jackie a meal and let her sleep on his bed while he took the couch. In the morning, she told him the rest of her story and how afraid she was that Leo would find her.

The usually callous, but loyal, fixer knew a few girls around town. He didn't have time for romantic entanglements but always had plenty of money and so he did what any other normal man would do in those circumstances. He figured that he didn't have the temperament to nursemaid the pretty, young, brown skinned whore. A girl who called herself only Dallas agreed to come over as soon as he called her. She was a tall, blond beauty who worked free lance. She hit it off with Jackie right away and nursed her for three days without charge. She made it clear to Jake that she was off the clock and he received no side benefits from her constant presence except the right to sleep on his own couch and the pleasure of having two beautiful, scantily clad women around his suite all day.

Something about Jackie's story really irked him. Betrayal was, to him, the worse of all sins. And Jackie was so afraid of what Leo and Taquan would do to her that she wouldn't go out of the hotel. He decided that he would have to do something.

About three in the morning, there was the customary knock on the door to Leo's seraglio. It was a coded knock that Jackie knew well. Jake and two of his trusted men had waited in the basement garage until they were sure that both Taquan and Leo were there. Jackie was with them since Jake had decided that seeing what went down would be the only thing that would clear her mind of fear.

When the door was opened by Luanda, she was met by three men holding two sawed off shotguns and a 9 millimeter, automatic pistol. She quietly stepped back. Leo's voice called out, "Who the fuck is it?" His back was to the door and he was the last of the five men sitting around the poker table to know that gunmen had entered the room. While Leon and Curley held the card players at bay, Jake searched the bedrooms, rousting the occupants. One of them was Taquan.

Seeing the whores and johns herded into the room, Leo got courage and rose from his chair. "You don't know what the fuck you're doing asshole," he said in his most threatening voice. Jake nodded to Curly who advanced on the fat man and clocked him with the stock of his shotgun, knocking his trademark fedora onto the floor. Leo went down back into his chair with an anguished groan.

"Neither do you, asshole," Jake answered him.

When everyone, except Taquan, had been collected in a little semi-circle, sitting on the rug, the angered but wounded Leo as well, Jake put the pistol in his belt. Jackie had crept in behind Jake and his boys, and Taquan saw her for the first time. "It's the little lost whore," he said mockingly. "Just wait girl, we'll get you. You think that these white boys…"

That was all he got out. Jake shot out a fist and caught Taquan on the jaw. You could have turned off the TV set right there. He beat the man unmercifully. Taquan was making so much noise crashing into furniture, wailing and screaming as Jake punched, kicked and chopped at his body, that Leon edged himself over to the CD player and turned up the volume. When Taquan was lying motionless on the floor, Jake went over to him. Holding his face in place with one hand, he brought the handgrip of his pistol down on his teeth. He smashed them three times until he had knocked out all the ones in front. Taquan squirmed and moaned in pain, too abused to do anything to stop Jake's punishment of him. When he was done with the evil man's mouth, Jake turned his attentions to his hands. He grabbed one of Taquan's wrists and, placing his hand flat on the floor, proceeded to pummel it with the handle of the firearm until his bones were a mass of jelly. He then did the same to Taquan's left. When he recovered from his beating, the toothless former pimp wouldn't even be able to jerk off.

The sly, unprincipled man's mouth was a gurgle with blood when Jake stood up. He didn't want him to drown so he lifted his body and flipped him to his belly. He turned to Leo.

The fat man squirmed, believing that it was his turn, but Jake had no thought of beating the fat man to a pulp. He had asked around and learned that Leo was connected. He wanted to teach the gangster a lesson, not start a war. Taquan may have been a valuable employee, but he was still just a worker and not a boss. Leo would remember what Jake was capable of and calculate the profit and losses before he retaliated. Jake was counting on him not.

"In case you want to know," Jake told the glaring man, who had a small stream of blood running down his face from Curley's instructional blow, "my name is Jake. Ask around. People know me. I'm telling you right now, that if anyone fucks with Jackie again, and I mean anybody, next time it'll be you lying on the floor with your teeth and hands all busted up. And maybe I'll cut your balls off too. Clear?"

Leo, too angry to respond just nodded his head.

"Okay, fellows," Jake said to the amazed, frightened men, "go back to your fun. By the way, for all you guys playing poker, the deck is marked. I got it on very good authority."

Leo's face reddened with fierce anger. He looked at the sawed offs and decided that he would do nothing. Now, that is. But he would definitely check up on this Jake.

CHAPTER SIX
THE SWEET SMELL OF SUCCESS

As it turned out, Leo did check Jake out and nothing was ever heard from him. Jackie, overwhelmed with happiness and gratitude, offered to fuck Jake's brains out. Jake demurred and the young brown skinned girl went off to live with Dallas for a while to learn her trade. It was the only skill that she had and once she learned how much money Dallas made in a night, she would hear nothing about secretarial school or community college.

But Jake's resolution to remain on the high road didn't last long and Jackie became his favorite whore soon thereafter. No one ever bothered her and she never charged him a nickel, even when she stayed all night.

When, a few years later, Jake offered Jackie a million dollars to become a ponygirl for five months she jumped at it. First of all, there was the money. She could only dream of what she would do with it, but she knew that she would quit whoring, at least mostly. Secondly, there was the debt that she owed Jake. If it wasn't for him, she would probably be dead or wishing that she was. She felt that she owed him something.

But being a ponygirl had been much worse than she had ever expected. Leo had whipped her once, twice if you counted the time with his belt, and that was bad, but as a ponygirl, she was whipped dozens and dozens of times and by men who were expert at it. She had been hooded and rendered faceless, unable to take the smallest volitional movement without permission, deprived of her hands and voice and fucked over and over again. That part she didn't mind so much. She even found her ability to orgasm had reached a new, unimaginable height. And she had been taught to receive pleasure through her small, dainty star between her rear cheeks, something that Leo didn't permit his whores to do because he thought that it was 'dirty'.

Jackie had revolted when she first learned how bad being a ponygirl was going to be, but she had been subdued and beaten into obedience. She had learned to run and run and run until it became a source of joy to her, reminiscent of her high school days. And there was the million bucks. Every day she reminded herself that her life as a ponygirl was not permanent, that someday Jake would free her. When she returned to civilization, she would be richer than she had ever imagined.

However, as soon as Jackie had become used to her travails as a ponygirl, she had been handed over to her driver for the racing season. She had known that it was coming, but life under the dwarfish man who ruled her every action, had been excruciating. He had tormented her beyond belief until she was responsive to his every gesture and desire. He had trained her hard and beaten her when she lost. She thanked God that it was not often.

The pony, Chocolate, had won eleven out of fourteen races. As far as she was concerned, she could have won them all. But her driver, for some reason, had held her back. He had even put specially weighted boots on her and mounted a heavy, steel plate under the sulky cart to slow her down. He always gave her free rein when the race was almost over and impossible to win.

Giorgi, Chocolate's driver, knew what he was doing. He knew the ponygirl was special, one in a million. She had a heart that wouldn't quit and couldn't stand the sight of another ponygirl cart pulling ahead of them. But he had a plan for the Fall Tournament. He knew that Jackie would qualify. Eleven victories were plenty to put her in the tournament, but not so much that she would have too high a seed. Enough, though, so that she would be in the middle of the pack and not have to face the higher ranking ponies in her fist heats. He had a little money on his pony and wanted the odds to be good when she took the championship.

But there was another reason. Burnham, her owner, and his sidekick, the man they called Jake, had laid out their plan to challenge last year's 1500 champion, Lightning, in a claiming race at the end of the season. Lightning's driver was his brother, Jerzy. There was a fierce competition between them. Jerzy had won seven championships and he had won five. They had only raced against each other in the finals once and Jerzi had beaten him. He wanted Jerzi to be overconfident when it came to the match race. Until then, he would let Chocolate win just enough, and with just enough of a lead, so that it would appear that she was good, but maybe not great. Her championship in the 1500 would be seen as a kind of fluke.

The original idea was to have Chocolate and Lightning meet in the 1500 meter championship race and to make that the match race that Burnham wanted. But after they had registered Chocolate for the 1500, they had found out that Lightning was running the 3000 meter instead. Her owner, Axmail Grobgy, had changed her for some reason.

According to the Racing Commission rules, it was too late to change Chocolate's division.

And so the plan had morphed to win the 1500 meter championship and then challenge Lightning, sure to win the 3000 meter, in a special race held on the day after the championship races. But to do that, Chocolate had to train for the 3000 meter in secret while, at the same time, winning enough 1500 meter races to qualify for the tournament.

During the season, on the off days when the racing teams were home at Burnham's estate, Giorgi would have Chocolate brought over to the all but deserted practice track at night and train her for the longer, more strenuous race. He had to give it to the pony. She was strong and had plenty of endurance. She was putting in some pretty good times at 3000 meters. He wasn't sure that she was going to be fast enough to beat Lightning, but she would give the other pony a run for her money. Giorgi worked carefully all season to build up Chocolate's strength. That was another reason to have her wear the lead bottomed boots that he had had made and to weigh down the cart. Every 1500 meter race that she ran with the extra burden seemed longer and more difficult, giving her the training that she had missed by being on the road.

Of course, for appearances sake, he had to beat her severely following the three races she had lost. Everyone expected no less and there would have been surprise had he done otherwise. It was unfair to the pony, which had tried her hardest but had suffered under a severe handicap, not to mention the fact that he had held her back. But whoever said that life was supposed to be fair for ponygirls. The whole idea was an oxymoron.

Chocolate had finally fallen back asleep after her terrible dream and night of reminiscences. It was chilly when she was awoken by the sensation of her driver's pretty and amiable, blond haired slave girl's removal of her ponygirl blanket. As usual, she cooed and stroked Chocolate's breasts and belly before she released her bindings. Today was the last race day of the season, although Chocolate didn't know that. There was no need to keep ponygirls informed about anything. All they needed to know was to obey and to give their all, whether streaming down the dirt track hauling a cart or carriage behind them or sucking the pricks of their masters.

Ilona was a Latvian and she had been Giorgi's assistant for three seasons. She had large, pleasant breasts and curvaceous hips. She kept her long, blond hair in a braid behind her head. Unlike Natasha, Jerzi's servant, Ilona had not developed a resentment against the strange, woman-like creatures that she cared for. To her, they were beautiful and helpless, unable to feed themselves or go anywhere without guidance. They even needed help to void themselves of wastes. She didn't mind wiping their well toned, pretty asses or cleaning their hairless slits. And she made sure that she comforted them so that, as much as they could, they remained content with their special status.

Ilona led the tall, big boned pony out of her trailer and, after taking her into the woods to void, had her kneel in the middle of the encampment amidst a small enclosure formed by five foot high, black and white checkered, cloth panels. Her master, Giorgi, was still sleeping and it was her task to groom the pony. Making sure that her face was pointed away from her, Ilona released the clasps that held the pony's hood taut to her collar and pulled it over her head.

She had already brought out a bowl of hot water and some soap. She dipped her practiced hands into the water and she covered the pony's scalp with it. There was a minute stubble that had arisen from the day before. Ilona applied the soap to the pony's head and made a sheen of soapy water. She then took her razor and carefully stroked the pony's scalp, making long, careful paths along the soapy presence. The slave girl was an expert at it and she soon had the brown scalp denuded of all evidence of hair except for the long, full tail that sprung from the back of her head. She applied a lotion to the hairless scalp, massaging it in gently while whispering sweet, Latvian phrases into the pony's ears.

Chocolate enjoyed being groomed by the friendly, pretty, naked, blond girl. Her hands on her head felt wonderful, the only tactile sensation that her head would experience for the next 24 hours. It reminded her that she had been made into a ponygirl and not born as one. The shaving of her day's growth, however, always reminded her, quite starkly, that she was, in fact, now a ponygirl, regardless of what she once was. She was under the iron willed control of the men and had no rights. Her only choices were to obey or not to obey which was the same thing as saying to suffer or not to suffer.

It was hard to resist the impulse to turn her head and thank the pleasant, blond woman for her kindly efforts. Her gag was free, a necessity if the hood was to be removed, and her face was visible. She could turn and smile and say, "Thank you," and flash her pretty, brown eyes at the girl. But if she did, she knew that she would be horribly beaten. The girl was not so kindly as she would fail to report such a gross breach of ponygirl discipline. And it would be a terrible shock to the poor girl, like having your dog say, "Thanks," after you put his dish of food on the floor in front of him.

The second thing that Chocolate liked about being groomed everyday was that the girl would reach her hands across her shoulders and apply the same cream that she administered to her scalp onto her face. It was nice to be reminded that you had one. The girl's hands were gentle and warm and she smoothed them across Chocolate's cheeks, forehead, nose and chin until the moisturizing and disinfectant lotion was fully worked in. Her delicate fingers lifted the large, thick, golden ring in her nose and spread the lotion over her upper lip. The neoprene hood caused the pony's face to dry out and it was important not to let it get old and whither. Infections or sores could set in, causing the pony stress. And if the pony was under stress, it might not perform as well. And if the ponygirl under her charge did not perform well because she hadn't been groomed properly, she, Ilona would be beaten severely, or worse.

It was time for the hood to be reapplied. Yesterday had been a practice day and Chocolate had worn the black Neoprene hood that was standard on her estate. Today was a race day, and so Ilona applied the racing hood which was both black and white. She drew the long skein of dark brown hair through the little hole in the back of the hood and then stretched the pliant fabric until it fit over the pony's head. She then slid it down until the face was covered, adjusting it so that the mouth and nostrils were free and the large, golden ring in her nose was on the outside available for use. She shifted the hood until the tiny eyelets fit perfectly over the pony's eyes. She clipped it to the ponygirl collar, drawing it tight.

Ilona ran her hands over the pony's strong shoulders. She loved the feel of the butternut skin. She put some more lotion in her hands and, leaning against the pony's back, spreading her naked thighs on either side of her, began to rub the moisturizer over her large, firm breasts. Her own bare breasts were pressed up against the pony's strong back and she luxuriated in the feel of its warm flesh against them. She began to rub the pony's full, soft mounds slowly and gently, pinching and teasing the stiffened nipples. She whispered into the pony's ear, "Pretty *Shokoladniy*, beautiful *Shokoladniy*," giving the pony's name in Russian.

Even slave girls have their secrets, and one of Ilona's was the way that she received delight from the lovely, brown ponygirl every morning. Her master was asleep and they were behind the 5' tall, black and white curtains she had set up so that passers by would not see the pony's face while she groomed it. Most people thought that a ponygirl's hands were useless, but Ilona knew better. They may be confined and disused, but they were not disfunctional. She had gotten the idea when she had seen some ponies doing it in a field during a break between racing seasons. One pony had climbed up against another's back and placed her needful sex on the other pony's hands. She watched, amazed, as the bottom pony used its hands to stroke and caress the upper pony's slit. They remainjed cojoined until the upper pony began to shake and moan in orgasmic delight.

Ilona maneuvered her soft, hairless slit onto Chocolate's hands. She continued to stroke the pony's breasts, whispering its name tenderly. The pony responded, like it always did, and its hands began a soft caress of her pussy lips.

The young, blond haired slave girl hugged the body of the ponygirl close to her as she experienced the pleasure of its fingers manipulating her hot slit. She moaned with pleasure as her lusts rose steadily. "Ohhhhhh, *Shokoladniy*," she sighed as its fingers found her stiffened clit. "Yesssss, pretty ponygirl," she moaned. "Oh, yesssss. Yessssssss."

Chocolate had no shame or compunction about this use of her. She loved to hear the slave girl moan her name in Russian. From its sound, she had guesed its meaning in English and she thought it singularly appropriate given her brown skin. And the slave girl was so nice to her. When she was permitted, she brought her to exquisite orgasms several times a day. And she was always kind and gentle. And there was the fact that even this limited use of her hands reminded her that they were still a part of her, even though she hadn't seen them in months. And, if there was nothing else, there was the smooth, soft, expert hands of the slave girl that were massaging and caressing her breasts, the recipricating warmth of the slave girl's breasts against her back and the comforting feeling of being embraced by a caring human being.

Ilona's passions built up quickly. She knew that she shouldn't dawdle and there was always the chance of the master rising early and, peeking behind the curtains, seeing her committing an offense. Slave girls' orgasms belonged to their masters and only they could dictate when and how they were spent. Giorgi would beat her severely if her caught her.

Chocolate could feel the slave girl's embrace become more needful and she could hear her soft voice issue low, passionate moans. Her hands were slick with her moisture as she teased the slave girl's fevered quim and the caresses of her breasts and the feel of the slave girl's body against hers had sparked her own desires. Her bare pussy burned between her outsretched thighs. But, as a ponygirl, she had no right to demand a reciprocal handling of her slick slit. She would have to wait until someone, anyone, decided to give it attention.

Suddenly the slave girl's thighs gripped her sides more tightly, her hips began to rock and her arms circled around her, hugging her firmly. She uttered a low, happy groan and Chocolate knew that she was coming.

Ilona gripped tightly to the body of the powerful, brown skinned ponygirl as her pussy sent her wave after wave of delight. She bit her lips to keep her vocal celebrations of her pleasure inside her, but she could not prevent the groan. Her body shuddered and her thighs quaked. And then, having crested, her sex's contractions began to ebb. She continued to hold tightly to the cooperative pony until their echoes had completely faded.

Giving the ponygirl a grateful kiss on her shoulder and her breasts a final, gentle caress, Ilona resumed her morning duties, her body tingling with reminisence of her pleasurable climax.

Next, the pony needed to be fed. On race days, Ilona always placed a little honey in the pony's breakfast gruel. It was sitting in a covered bowl and she placed it in front of the pony so that she could eat it, giving the pony and affectionate rub on top of its hooded head.

Chocolate leaned over, crushing her breasts against her knees, her again useless hands bound behind her, and slurped the thick porridge from the bowl with delight. She already knew that it was racing day because she had been dressed in her shiny, black and white hood, but the sweet taste of her usually bland meal was confirmation. As a ponygirl, Chocolate had learned to take her pleasures where she could find them and when the porridge was gone, she carefully licked the bowl clean, consuming and enjoying every drop of the honeyed taste. When she was done, Ilona reinstalled her gag.

According to their morning ritual, next was the shaving of the pony's loins. When the bowl was removed from in front of her, Chocolate let herself be leaned back and she slid her legs out from under her. She knew what was coming, but never made a motion to change her position in anticipation until she felt the girl's gentle hands on her shoulders urging her back. Ponygirls were not supposed to know anything or do anything on their own. For all she knew, as unlikely as it was, there might be a different plan for today. A movement not permitted could result in a beating.

Ilona had another bowl of hot water next to her that she had kept covered. While the pony lay with her back on the grass, spreading her legs widely, Ilona shaved her pudenda clean. There was nothing that reminded Chocolate of her subservience to her masters more than the act of spreading her knees wide and having her pussy shaved every day. Her slit was open to all who desired it, not hers to control or touch. Every day she had to yield up her sex to either her driver's slave girl or, when she was back in the ponygirl barn, to one of the male grooms or trainers and submit to this ritual. She didn't know it, but she was reacting precisely according to the intent of the procedure. It would be more convenient to apply a permanent depilitating agent on her loins and have done with it. Having the pony spread her legs wide and submit to the careful and thorough handling of her cunt every morning was meant to remind her of her lack of control over her body. Her pussy was not for her to touch, but for her masters and those who they permitted the liberty. It was to remain fully visible to all, a prominent aspect of her features. Most slave girls had their pudenda shaved as well, for this same reason, but at least, after their training, they got to do it themselves.

The slave girls, generally speaking, feared and abhorred the ponygirls. They were strong and muscular and appeared otherworldly and were a living reminder of what cruelties their masters were capable of. Many a slave girl had been threatened to be reduced to ponygirl status. Although it rarely occurred, the thought that it might happen to them made the imbonded girls realize that things really could be worse than being a sexual thrall.

One of Ilona's duties was to see to the sexual needs of the ponygirl. On most mornings, just as when the pony lived in the pony barn, this would be the occasion of the pony's first orgasm of the day. In the pony barn, a groom or a trainer would bring the pony to a body shuddering orgasm every morning with his hand, his mouth or his prick, as the impulse took him. Ilona didn't have a prick although she sometimes used a large black dildo strapped to her waist to bring the ponygirl to completion. That was usually in the afternoons after a training run, or in the evening while her master watched for his amusement. In the mornings, Ilona used, generally, her hands or her mouth to bring delight to the animal. Since this was a race day, *Shokoladniy* would not be permitted an orgasm until and unless it won its race.

Giorgi's philosophy regarding the sexual lives of ponygirls was different than Jerzy's. While Jerzy believed that a near total deprivation of orgasms brought out the competitive nature of the ponies the best, Giorgi's concept was that by singling the race day out as a day of denial, the pony would be all the more eager to perform at its best to insure that it did not go the whole day without relief. Keeping the ponygirl at a sexual peak, driving her need to orgasm by delivering it several times a day, made the absence of the orgasm more difficult to bear. And so Ilona's instructions were to caress, fuck or suck the ponygirl's hairless twat to completion often during he course of the day or night. Except on race day, when she would drive her just to the edge and no further, stoking her needs into an intolerable craving.

Ilona ran her soft hands over the insides of Chocolate's widespread thighs. Like most slave girls, Ilona had never handled another woman's sex or suckled a breast before she was kidnapped and made a slave. It was a standard training protocol to teach them to enjoy it. As a ponygirl driver's servant, Ilona had licked and kissed many a soft, hairless quim and she had no compunction about doing it today. While a ponygirl was no longer a woman, she had a woman's parts. Her own slash would dilate and moisten as she did it, renewing her own desire for sexual fulfillment. And one of the good things about race day was that since Giorgi would not fuck the ponygirl, he would probably, this morning, fuck her.

The blond haired slave girl lifted the pony's strong, well toned legs and placed them over her shoulders. She leaned over and ran her tongue the length of the pony's smooth, brown slash. She could feel its reactions as its legs shuddered. She did it again and the pony's back arched and it raised its hips to better receive the young girl's oral attention. Its gash was already moist and dilated from Ilona's prior handling. When the slave girl seized the nubbin at Chocolate's pussy's apex between her lips, the pony moaned and shifted its hips in response. The blond slave continued to suckle at the small point of flesh until it hardened under her ministrations. Circling her hands around the pony's thighs, she delved her agile tongue deep inside its crevasse and lashed at the moist, pungent walls until the pony groaned with desire. And then, giving the pleasure bud a little kiss, she withdrew her services and gently allowed the pony's legs to fall to the ground.

Chocolate's whole body was trembling with need. Her mind was flush with pleasure and the unfulfilled promise of the hot tongue that had enflamed her. She tried to bring her thighs together, but the slave girl knelt between them. She gave out a great sigh and then lay prone and still.

When the pony had cooled, Ilona stood and clapped her hands twice. It was the signal for the ponygirl to rise. When Chocolate had risen to her feet, she was brought to the overhead shower and Ilona proceeded to wash every inch of her body. She took special care to shampoo and rinse the pretty ponytail that emerged from the back of her hood and to clean and dry her valuable ponygirl feet. She even removed her gag and brushed her teeth. Chocolate enjoyed the feel of the girl's soft hands on her body and the clean, tight feeling her skin had when the cool shower was completed.

Having seen to the pony's hygienic needs, Ilona went and retrieved its pony boots. Once they were on, she led it to a 6' high pole that stood in the ground and fastened the back of its collar near the top with a short chain. Smiling at the pretty, helpless ponygirl, she placed her hand between its thighs and caressed it once more, until she felt that its pussy was again loose and wet. She left the pony standing there while she got her master's breakfast.

Whereas the ponies' breakfast of specially brewed gook containing vitamins and nutrients considered essential for a healthy ponygirl was delivered each morning by a cart pulled by two of the estate's work ponies, the master's breakfast was prepared at a chuck wagon on the edge of the pony encampment. Ilona scurried away to retrieve it. Before she did so, however, she was careful to adorn herself with a slave gag that covered the lower portion of her face. She dutifully filled her mouth with its thick, leather prong and locked it behind her head. No slave girl was permitted to run around ungagged. Communication between slave girls was frowned upon, especially during racing season where news of a strained muscle or a blistered toe could effect, not only the strategy of an opposing ponygirl team, but also the odds for betting. Gossip between slave girls could spread rumors and find its way to the wrong ears.

There was a line of naked and gagged slave girls at the chuck wagon retrieving their masters' breakfasts. Ilona bounced nervously on her bare toes as she waited for the line to go down. She knew that her master would be rising very soon and she wanted to have his breakfast waiting for him. Unlike Jerzi, Giorgi was not a particularly cruel master, but he did have a mean streak in him, as all masters did. It seemed to just naturally develop in them after years of expecting immediate, precise and full satisfaction of their needs and desires.

In fact, the dwarfish ponygirl driver was just emerging from his trailer. He noted with annoyance that his breakfast was not ready as he stretched himself to his full but still diminutive height, getting the kinks out of his back. He was dressed in his racing regalia, shiny silk pants and blouse, colored black and white like the pony's hood, but in quarters rather than in hemispheres. He saw the ponygirl properly mounted and ready for her morning's warm up run with satisfaction. He decided to wait until later as to whether to give his slave a beating or not.

Giorgi strolled leisurely over to where Chocolate stood patiently awaiting the day's activities. He loved her brown skin. Not many of the ponies were brown skinned, but that was changing. The true delectability of colored flesh had been a recent discovery in the small former republic, and black, brown and tan girls were coming in to the country now in growing numbers. One of the estates fielded an all Latino cabriolet six pony team from Nicaragua. Brown skinned, Indian, peasant girls, grown tall and strong up in the mountains, were well adapted to pulling a heavy pony carriage. And two of the drivers for Burnham's estate had servants whose skin was as black as tar. He had fucked them and they were very good. He had made a note to consider selling Ilona and getting one of the black beauties.

Giorgi was all of four feet tall and the brown skinned ponygirl towered over him. Sometimes he thought it funny that a small man like him could so easily control a huge animal like her. But obedience had been firmly drilled into the heads of the former women, and size was no measure of the cruelty that one could deliver. He ran his hands up the pony's graceful, smooth, thick thighs. He admired her strength. She had done well. And she would do better. He placed his hand between her thighs and the pony, which, because of its uplifted chin, sensed him more than saw him, spread its legs obediently to give him access. He began to stroke its delicate, brown love lips until he could see moisture develop between them. Its hips sought his hand, pressing its loins against it. The pony was in need, as it should be. He wiped his hand on its belly and walked away.

Ilona arrived panting and out of breath with his breakfast. Her large breasts swayed and shimmered delightfully as she proffered it to him. It was a covered plate containing several pieces of bacon, scrambled eggs and roasted potatoes. He motioned for her to put it on the small table by his chair and she rushed off to get his coffee from the pot warming by the fire. When she returned and placed the cup on the table, he snapped his fingers and pointed to the ground. The pretty, anxious slave girl fell to her knees. He made another motion with her hand and she turned away from him and bent over, proffering her plump, soft, white rear globes. He'd decided that she was getting slack and needed a refresher on her duties. There was always a long, thin switch ready by the trailer door and he picked it up.

Giorgi, to Ilona's dismay, gave the switch a ride through the air before he put it to use. The sound of the whip cutting the air was a familiar, dismal one to the slave girl. Her life was spent in fear of abuse. Although she hated the small man who was her master, she never showed it. That would be an invitation to even worse abuse. But she yearned for her home, her former life, her freedom. No slave girl that she knew of had ever escaped. A few times she had seen the abused and mangled bodies of slave girls who had tried brought back for display purposes, and others suffer a heinous torture before an assembled, distraught crowd of her sister slaves before, if she was still capable, being returned to her duties. But she could hope and pray. In the meantime, she would try and avoid moments like these as best she could and take what joy she could from his sexual use of her, the only joy that she really had.

Satisfied that the whip was operational, not that there was any doubt, Giorgi brought it down fiercely on the smooth round surface of Ilona's ass. She howled behind her gag as the fiery sensations shot through her. Her hands were clenched tightly and her body tense as she readied herself for another. Her expectation was proved prescient when a second blow landed across her rear mounds as forceful and as painful as the first. Her eyes tearing from the pain, she wondered how many more that the evil man would give her. Her answer came as a third and final slice of the fiercely wielded instrument bit into her flesh.

Ilona just knelt in the grass, crying, her head hung down, her rump burning as Giorgi peaceably and contentedly ate his breakfast. He looked casually at the long, red lines he had created and wondered idly whether the flesh of the black skinned girls bruised so nicely. He would have to ask his friend, Pietrov, who had one of those girls, for a demonstration.

Chocolate's warm up run went off without incident. When she came back, Ilona washed her down and massaged her legs and thighs. The track had been mushy and soft, giving Giorgi second thoughts about today's strategy. The pony needed practice running on a muddy track in case it was faced with one in the tournament. And if he used the weighted boots in the mud, he increased the pony's chance of injury. Even though it was an away match and the pony had not had her 3000 meter workouts for two days, he decided that he would let her run all out.

In the meantime, there was some time to kill before the races started. The vision of his slave girl's posterior striped with lacerations had stayed with him all morning. He was sitting in his little chair outside of his trailer and watching it now with intense interest. She was kneeling, mouthing the ponygirl to excitement. She had her own legs spread enticingly and he could see her plump, hairless love lips gaping open and slick with her own lust.

Chocolate was lying on the grass, her legs extended, her chest rising and falling rapidly as her passions grew. Every time the pony came close to completion, the slave girl withdrew her tongue from her pussy and waited for her to cool, stroking her thighs and belly. The ponygirl wore the angry, black mastiff etched into her skin, her owner's symbol, and it seemed to vibrate as her tummy shivered with need. She bit down hard on the leather covered steel bit in her mouth in frustration. When the brown skinned creature finally relaxed, giving out a deep sigh, Ilona began again.

After the slave girl's third delivery of foreshortened cunnilingus, he called her over to him and had her kneel before him, crouched over, her ass raised and her knees spread. His cock was already hard from watching the girl on pony display. He stood and approached his slave girl from behind and undid his fly. Before entering her, he ran his gnarled hands over the taut, smooth skin of her rear, tracing the lines that he had put there this morning. Her long, golden braid had fallen to one side and was resting on her left shoulder. The pale, almost translucent skin of her back was stretched and taut and he could see the knots of her spine curving in an arc from the top of her ass to her neck. He wondered idly how many times he had fucked her. Two hundred? Three? Four? At least once a day for a year and a half. She was a delectable slut, but she had been with him too long. He could get about twenty thousand kronskis for her down in Dlitski, maybe more if her could get another driver interested in her. She was good at handling the ponies. He would have the entire winter to break in a new slave. Well, he didn't have to decide now, especially with her still quite delectable ass poised to receive him.

Giorgi pressed his tube of meat at the girl's excited quim. He slid in easily, making her moan. Her pussy's walls gripped him tightly, as she had been taught. He gave a great sigh as the pressure on his cock caused a surge of pleasure to flow through him. He began a slow, patient motion within her. There was plenty of time to kill and there was no reason to rush things.

Chocolate was still lying on her back in the grass. Due to the tiny holes in her hood and the uplift of her chin caused by her collar, all she could see was a small section of the cloudy sky above her. Her nerves were on edge from her cunnilingus interruptus. She heard the slave girl moan and knew that she was receiving the benefit of her driver's cock. Ilona had clipped her ankle boots together before she answered her master's summons and the pony squeezed her thighs together in frustration. She closed her eyes to try and put her need away, but the sounds of the coitus several feet away from her was keeping her lust on a boil. She prayed that her driver would let her win the race today. The track had been slippery and she had had a little trouble at the start and in keeping her feet steady as she planted them after each long, intense stride. She knew that her intensive need for sexual release was artificially driven, that the men had done this to her, but it didn't really matter if her crazed desire for the pleasure of a cock in her burning canal was due to her lascivious nature or because of what they had trained her into. The need was real either way.

Ilona kept up a continuous, low pitched hum of satisfaction as her master rode her hungry sheath. Her prayer had been answered. The presence of her master's cock and her impending orgasm were compensation for the lashing he had given her this morning. He was ugly and deformed, but he knew how to use his prick. She didn't know how long she would be his servant, but she hoped it was for a long while. She had been a slave girl at an estate when he had bought her. Serving different men every day, being subject to their varying demands, not being sure of how to best satisfy them and suffering the results if she failed, was a hard, uncertain life. Since Giorgi had owned her, she had had just one man to satisfy for the most part, except when he loaned her to the other drivers. And that didn't happen too often. And she loved serving the ponygirls, having free rein with their bodies, caring for them like huge, silent pets. Besides, a new owner would mean a constant series of beatings until she was trained to satisfy him in the ways that he wanted. She determined to work harder to satisfy her master. She wouldn't make the same mistake that she made this morning again. The last thing that she wanted was to be sold.

Giorgi let his cock wander along the trail of the slave girl's crevasse for quite some time. She came after about ten minutes, her body shuddering, her moaning growing louder and more intense, but, to her credit, she never shifted position, never ceased her pussy's counterstrokes to his motion. His hands rested on her buttocks as he rocked his hips back and forth slowly. His cock was sending him a mesmerizing flow of delectable sensations. He felt like he could continue at this all day. But that was just it. Ilona was a good fuck, but they were almost like an old married couple, achieving satisfaction without passion. No, he thought as he plowed her cunt, she would have to go. As soon as the season was over, she would be sold.

After about another five minutes of constant, low keyed motions, Giorgi decided that it was time to bring his lusts to a boil. He began to stroke his cock back and forth within his slave's canal faster and faster. He could feel his testes tighten and his blood rise. The girl's moans increased as did his tempo and she was moaning louder now, receiving her own delight. Giorgi looked down and saw her small, dainty rear entrance gaping. He suddenly felt the desire to penetrate it, to finish himself off within her bowels. The girl gasped as he withdrew his meat quickly from her slit and pointed it at the brown star between her rear cheeks. Her pussy's discharges on his cock provided ample lubrication and as he thrust his hips forward, his thick cock slipped right in. He could feel the tight pressure of her anal muscles around his shaft as he sawed back and forth along it. Her insides were hot and soft as if his prick had been dipped into a relaxing, equatorial sea. He arched his back and closed his eyes. His cock was readying its explosion and he reveled in being in the space between control and the loss of it. He groaned as his pole began to throb and jerk within the slave girl's bowels. His hands gripped her hips as if he needed to steady himself in a storm. A deep roar arose from his throat as his fervent prick continued to jet spurt after spurt of his spewm within her.

Ilona was surprised when she felt the master's thick, hard prong vacate her excited channel. But when she felt it return to her body through her narrow, rear aperture, her pussy exploded with pleasure. Each stroke of the man's meat across the tender, sensitive ring produced a matching, exquisite contraction of her womb. "Oh, god! Oh, god! Oh, god," she thought deliriously as her orgasm went on and on. The eruption of her master's prick inside her and his excited, passionate noises drove her pussy's convulsions deeper and harder. It was only when his motions slowed to a halt and she heard his long, satisfied sigh that they began to subside.

When her master exited her, Ilona dutifully ran for a bowl of hot water and a cloth to clean him off. As per his standing instructions, she gave his tool a gentle suckle as a signal that it was free of her wastes.

About an hour after lunch, it was time for the pony parade. All of the day's contestants lined up and displayed themselves before the crowded grandstand while receiving polite, or in some cases, such as Chocolate's, excited applause. The sulky races were last and so after the parade, Chocolate was returned to the campsite to await her turn to run.

Giorgi didn't bother with removing her racing harness, but she was released from her traces until it was time to go. She stood at her post dutifully, receiving the occasional caress to heighten her preparedness until her driver signaled that it was time.

Chocolate was appropriately anxious and worked up as she was eased back in between the poles that ran on the outside of the sulky cart. They were attached to the belt of her harness and then the straps that distributed the weight of her burden across her back and shoulders. She had listened to the noise of the distant race track, the trumpets, the roars of the crowd, nervously rubbing her strong thighs together, taking little, dancing steps on her pony boots. She was wearing a tall, black plume on her hood and the cart was decorated with white and black ribbons. Ilona had spent a good deal of her time polishing and cleaning it. Giorgi stepped in front of her and gave each of her breasts a strong, passion inducing suckle as her stroked her slit. Her moans signaled her readiness.

It was always a thrill to the chocolate pony to enter the track just before a race. Unlike other times, when it was crowded with teams warming up, or during the pre-race parade, it was empty except for the pony and cart belonging to the other team. Bright, colorful flags flew around it and over the large, crowded grandstand. She could hear the excited murmur of the crowd as she did a warm up lap. The faces of the audience were just a blur as she looked at them through the small holes in her hood, but she could see the fine clothes and happy demeanors of the people who crowded the rail.

Chocolate, of course, had no idea who the owner of the estate was that they were competing against today. The other pony wore an orange and blue hood with a bright orange plume over its head. Chocolate always tried to scope the other pony out. Was she big? Were her thighs thick or sleek? Did it look like she had what it takes? But the sight challenged pony could usually only get mere glances at it.

The track was muddy and had been churned up by the earlier races. Workers had thrown absorbent sand out on the worst spots, tamping it down with special tools. But, it had rained for long and hard the night before and the normally smooth and firm track was slippery and treacherous.

Giorgi looked over at the opposing pony as he guided Chocolate up to the starting line. It was tall and pale skinned with a long, blond tail emerging from its hood. Its name was *Ninotchka* and she was a good runner. Two years ago, in the spring season, he had lost to her. The reports that he had seen showed that it had lost just a little bit of speed but that it was a good mudder. She had won ten races this fall and there was a good chance that they would see it again in one of their heats in the Fall Tournament. He knew her driver well, too. Jakob, one of the few Jewish drivers, had a reputation for jumping out early and using his very capable blocking skills to keep it. Strictly speaking, blocking was an illegal tactic, and if you caused your pony or cart to make contact with your competitor's, you would face disqualification. But Jakob had it down to an art just like he had eyes in the back of his head.

The ponies pawed the soft earth nervously as they waited for the ready signal. At the ready flag's signal, the crowd hushed and the ponies' bodies tensed. Starting position was one leg back, anchored firmly in the dirt, the other forward, knee bent, toe planted. *Ninotchka* was one of the few lefty runners, its left boot forward. Chocolate, like most of the others, kept her right foot ahead. There was a small breeze and the ponies' plumes shuffled above them.

Giorgi gripped the reins tightly. The gun sounded and they were off.

To Chocolate's dismay, her right foot sank deeply into the track as she tried to push off on it and she slipped to her knees. Giorgi roared his unhappiness and gave her a brutal crack of his whip across her shoulders. It took five, long, wasteful seconds for the pony to rise to its feet and take off down the track. *Ninotchka* was already almost five lengths ahead.

A five length lead might be something easily overcome in the longer 3000 meter, but in the faster 1500 meter, where speed was everything, it was almost always fatal. There had been a loud moan from the crowd as they saw the brown skinned pony fall and many a patron threw his or her program down in disgust and tore up their betting ticket.

But the race was not yet over. Chocolate was mortified at her error and fiercely despondent at her apparent loss of the opportunity of victory. She knew that she would suffer a brutal punishment for her slip, but more importantly, for her, she would be denied any respite from her gnawing sexual need. By the time that she got up to full speed, *Ninotchka* had an advantage of about seven lengths. It looked hopeless. But her thoughts went back to her dream of the night before. She remembered churning her legs helplessly as the huge, demonic hand pursued her. She vowed that it would not happen again

Fans of ponygirl racing, like any other sport, often argue about the best moments, the historic races, the, "If only I had been there," contests. There was the Pandora/Starburst 3000 meter in '98, the Juniper/Dazzler 1500 contest in '04 in which both ponies set world records.

Some argued that the Berensky/Krakov estates' landau match, 18 ponies in six rows of three pulling the two huge, lumbering carriages for 6000 meters in the midst of a torrential downpour, was the greatest. Three of the ponies had finished the race despite agonizing, career ending injuries.

The *Ninotchka/Shokoladniy* race is considered to have been right up there. No one believed that the clumsy, brown skinned pony would ever catch the swift, experienced blond one. But those that doubted had not seen Chocolate's medal winning run when she was a seventeen year old high school junior named Jackie.

Chocolate's mind raged with the need for victory. Even Giorgi was surprised as the determination and world class grit that she showed. At the ¼ turn, *Ninotchka* still maintained a formidable lead. But by the half, *Shokoladniy* had reduced it to four lengths. At the ¾ pole, it had become a real race.

Jakob had, characteristically and understandably, maintained his pony at a moderate cruise once he saw the brown pony fall. It was a sloppy track and even though *Ninotchka* ran well in those kinds of conditions, the tournament was a week away and he certainly didn't want to risk an injury. Even as the frantically churning *Shokoladniy* began to close the gap, he was not concerned, since *Ninotchka* had plenty left and the other pony's resources were being severly strained. When his lead was down to two lengths, he began to get nervous and yanked the reins indicating a desire for more speed. But the other pony kept on coming.

Both drivers were frantically laying on their long, narrow dressage whips as the contestants made the near turn and headed down the home stretch. The lead was exchanged three times. The crowd was roaring with excitement reserved usually for championship bouts. A few betters were desparately crawling around the floor looking for their torn ducats, being pushed and shoved and stepped on by the manic crowd.

On the walls of many a ponygirl racecourse clubhouse, the only place that ponygirl pictures are permitted to be displayed, you can still see the print of the photo finish. Both ponies' bodies are covered with the mud of the track from their waists down. The driver's faces are contorted with their efforts to force just one more ounce of effort from their charges. Chocolate's right foot had just struck a large puddle and there is a huge spray of mud as her foot landed. Her large breasts are flung out as if seeking victory. It takes the assistance of a magnifying glass, but if you use one, you can just see the edge of Chocolate's black and white forward leaning forehead crossing the finish line ahead of the orange and blue forehead of *Ninotchka*.

The crowd hushed as they watched the ponies cross the finish line. To the naked eye, the race had ended in a dead tie. The intensity of the drama that they had just witnessed flowed though the crowd like static electricity. Men and women laughed nervously as they waited for the officials' decision.

Chocolate was sure that she had lost. Her body ached with misery as she was taken through her cool off lap. She was actually sobbing as she passed the halfway pole. She had given it everything that she had. Her thighs ached and her lungs were still heaving in painful paroxysms. Giorgi leaned back in the sulky chair, not sure what he had just seen. No pony he had ever driven could have done what

Chocolate had just done. He hoped and prayed that she had won because it would be a sin to have to beat her after that performance.

The announcement of the winner by decision of the racing officials up in the booth flashed on the tote board when Chocolate was trotting dismally past the ¾ pole. It was signaled by the roar of the crowd. Giorgi couldn't see it from where he was, but it was a moment that he would remember for the rest of his life. The crowd noise drowned out the announcer's voice from the loudspeakers. But he knew that Chocolate had won the day when he heard the crowd start to chant, faintly, at first, among the general pandemonium, but then louder and louder as if every voice among the 2,156 people officially present had joined in: "*Sho-ko-lad-niy! Sho-ko-lad-niy! Sho-ko-lad-niy! Sho-ko-lad-niy!*"

Chocolate heard it too. Her hooded head raised and a surge of joy burst through her. Her heart began to pound and, for the first time since she had become a ponygirl, she felt like shouting with glee. Giorgi gave the pony's reins a jolt, signaling the pony to speed. Chocolate received it with happiness and began to pump and drive her legs as if the race had never happened. They sped by the grandstand as the crowd's chants became louder and louder. It continued as they made their way once more around the track, the mud splashing as Chocolate pounded away with her boots. Her whole body celebrated her joy and she felt like she could keep running until she wore her feet into truncated stubs and died. As they passed the grandstand once more, Giorgi waived his silky, black and white cap at the crowd initiating another round of manic cheers.

Jake had been watching from one of the boxes on the upper level. He always bet on Jackie and he had won a small bundle. He was too amazed at what he had just seen to think about that now. The whore from Chicago had just become the toast of Kalikastan. Within the hour, newspapers on the streets of Dlitski would be out in special editions detailing the historic race. While no pictures of the ponygirl races were allowed, their results, disguised as horseracing reports, were closely followed throughout the country.

"Fuck," he thought. While he was proud of the pony's results, it would certainly complicate his job of getting her out of the country after the Lightning match race. But he had to admit that it was one of the most amazing things he had ever seen. Irkut, Chocolate's trainer, had been sitting in the box with him and Jake thought that the sixtyish man was going to have a heart attack.

Giorgi eased Chocolate into the winner's circle. The small area was mobbed with excited well wishers yearning to touch the flesh of the heroic pony. A circle of security men was straining to keep them out. Jakob had halted his still recovering pony in front of the grandstand, a thing not usually done since the spotlight ordinarily went to the winner, and jumped off his cart. He rushed into the winner's circle and threw his arms around his fellow dwarf who had just descended from his. Now that picture you can still get. And if you examine it closely, you can just see a glimpse of what might be a sweaty, firm, brown rump on the edge. It's cropped out in later prints, but it's in the original carried by the sports pages in Dlitski. Only the cognoscenti would know what it was.

It was an exhausted and thrilled Chocolate who trotted down the narrow lanes of the ponygirl encampment, her neck encircled with the proof of her victory, a garland of bright red, yellow and purple flowers. Ilona, who had been left gagged and kneeling in the center of the camp, her wrists and ankles bound, had not known what to make of the loud cheers that she heard from the distant race track. When she saw the mud spattered, black and white hooded pony, bedecked with the circlet of victory, come trotting into the camp site, she knew that her pony had won. Giorgi leapt off of the cart, his face alight with pride. He unbound the happy slave girl and ordered her to unleash the pony. Men from the other camps came running in as word of Chocolate's tremendous victory spread. Bottles were broken out and hands clapped the back of the diminutive driver.

Giorgi did not wait for Ilona to remove Chocolate's racing harness. Taking her by the shoulders, he led her to the ground. He knelt between her muddy, outstretched legs and, after running his hands over the inner portions of her splattered thighs, bent over and put his mouth to her sex.

Chocolate welcomed the hot mouth on her loins. She didn't care that a large circle of trainers and grooms had assembled and were watching her being driven to lust. She closed her eyes behind her hood and reveled in the rough tongue that dragged along the length of her labia. She spread her legs wide and pushed her hips up the better to receive her master's adorations. Her heart was still beating wildly from her extraordinary performance, but soon the rhythms of her driver's tongue running up and down her slit, tickling her needy nubbin, took possession of her body. Giorgi bit down on her hardened bud, sending a mixed message of pain and pleasure through her, driving her passions higher. He sucked at it and then tickled it with his tongue until she groaned behind her steel bit.

Chocolate's body was electrified. Waves of pleasure ran through her. She arched her back and drew her knees up as she felt her orgasm pending. When it came, she moaned wildly and her body shook. A series of hard, exquisite contractions rocked her crevasse. Her nipples felt hard as rocks and her mind clouded over. The dwarf just went on and on tormenting her slit with his tongue. Her fading orgasm gave way to a second, which made her body shudder as she dug the heels of her ponygirl boots deeply into the ground.

The ponygirl was on the way to her third orgasm when the dwarf drew his head back from her loins. She gave a moan of frustration which turned to a moan of lust as he knelt between her legs, drew his thick, man sized cock from his racing pants and mounted her. The feel of the hard meat filling her gorge was overwhelming. The universe reduced itself to the contact between his prick and her yearning sheath. She began to moan rhythmically as the steel like pole ran its course back and forth within her. She came again and, as her pussy quaked with its convulsions, she wrapped her long, powerful legs around the back of her master's thighs and drove his cock deeper inside. She felt his cock jerk and pulse within her and she welcomed it with a powerful thrust of her hips.

When Giorgi rose from the moaning, satisfied pony, the crowd of onlookers gave out a big cheer. He was handed a bottle and he took a big gulp. The Fall Season had ended spectacularly for him and the chocolate pony. He would have to forget getting good odds at the tournament since all the money now would be on the crowd favorite, *Shokoladniy*.

Chocolate lay on the grass, her legs ajar, catching her breath, grateful for the chance at ecstasy. The crowd stumbled around her as the men of the encampment strained to give their personal congratulations to her master. She felt a hundred eyes on her naked, recumbent form, her ample breasts, her dilated and now gooey, hairless slit, her grotesquely tattooed torso, but she did not care. She had come a long way since she had timidly shown her pussy to Leo's friends that night years ago. She knew that she was in for an afternoon and evening of repeated, exquisite pleasure. She also knew now that she had been in the hands of a master. All of her training, the whips, the sexual deprivation, even the countless orgasms she had enjoyed at his or his slave girl's hands had molded her to the creature that performed for the crowd today. She was ready, she knew, to run the race of her life. She had been told by Jake before her ordeal as a ponygirl had begun about the proposed and hoped for match race against Maddy, the pony they called Lightning. She felt like she could beat any pony alive. And then she could go home.

End of Book Eight